The Lonely Man

Also by Faith Baldwin
In Thorndike Large Print

GIVE LOVE THE AIR
HE MARRIED A DOCTOR
THE HEART HAS WINGS
NO PRIVATE HEAVEN

The Lonely Man

Faith Baldwin

Thorndike Press • Thorndike, Maine

Library of Congress Cataloging in Publication Data:

Baldwin, Faith, 1893–1978.
  The lonely man.

  1. Large type books.   I. Title.
  [PS3505.U97L6 1987]   813'.52   87-5043
  ISBN 0-89621-789-2 (alk. paper)

Large Print edition available by arrangement with Henry Holt and
Co., Inc.

Cover design by Abby Trudeau.
Cover illustration by Deborah Pompano.

Dedicated
to the Regulars and Irregulars of
the Elm Street Saturday Lunch Club
with love

Foreword

Not many people read forewords and it is no longer fashionable to write them. Besides, did not Disraeli advise: "Never explain . . . "?

Yet I must explain Seascape. It is not (nor is Stone's River) on any map in any atlas I possess. However, when this book was half written, I found, in a village of another name, a subdivision called Seascape. It is not the Seascape of this story.

Seascape could be a number of villages; it has dunes and sea, and so have many places along our coast line. Think of it as you will and where you wish.

I selected the name of my lonely man from among my ancestral names. Actually I long ago wrote two books about people named Condit. My principal character in the first one was a doctor; he had a son, also a doctor. But when I reluctantly reread these books I found that the present Condit could not be related to my original characters. I did not give a son to

7

the younger doctor Condit.

As for Lister Memorial Hospital in New York, I created it in other books. I've written a number of novels dealing with doctors, nurses, and hospitals but none in some twenty years.

In this one I do not intend to deal with new procedures, medicines, or the intricate problems of diagnosis and prognosis; all these are currently presented in other people's novels, in nonfiction, in the motion pictures and on the television screen. This time I am more interested in the man himself and what living his profession does to him rather than what his profession brings to others.

I am indebted to a Labrador named Sheba, whom I know quite well, and to David S. Brown, M.D. – to the one for the understanding of her noble breed, to the other for a conversation which afforded me the theme of this book. I ask his forgiveness if he doesn't enjoy it. Which is very likely. . . .

F.B.
Norwalk, Connecticut

Chapter One

In the blue and charcoal dusk of early spring, the Labrador had been swimming. A few minutes ago he had retrieved a flung stick, bringing it back to the beach and the personage who had thrown it for him. He swam strongly, lifting his great paws as though they were fists, putting them down, and spreading them. Now he was exploring the beach.

He was an adult dog, not yet middle-aged, black as a starless night, curious, receptive, and to a degree self-controlled and sedate, being conscious of responsibility. When he went along on house calls, he sat erect and quiet in the car, responding to the greetings of two-legged people — both those who recognized him and those who did not. To the importunities of four-legged individuals he paid little, if any, attention.

Occasionally, when he was in his own yard or on the road, he was accosted by those inferior breeds; these he avoided carefully but with a dignity not to be confused with cowardice. If attacked he was formidable.

Often he went along on hospital visits, too. The hospital was some distance from his home and going there entailed a long waiting period, during which he often slept.

He was not permitted in the office or waiting room which were attached to the house where he lived. This was the edict of the woman who also lived there and to whom he accorded tolerance and a certain amount of respect. He neither liked nor disliked her. But he regretted not being able to speak to the many patients who came and went – unless, of course, he happened to be outside. During office hours, if he was in the house, he spent much of his time with Mrs. Parker, the housekeeper, a sensible woman for whom he had a high regard. Unless he was otherwise engaged, he gravely escorted her to her car evenings, after dinner and washing-up.

Now he stopped where the crescent beach curved and waded again into the cold, therefore delightful, water. There was still sufficient light by which to observe, in the little pools left by a receding tide, the quicksilver movements of small fish. He had long since learned the hard way not to try to catch them. It is foolish to attempt the impossible. Now and then he reflectively stirred the water with a paw and contemplated the result.

Jonathan Condit, walking down the beach, was aware of a number of things: of his fatigue, which he did not conflict with the knowledge that his body was strong and his muscles hard; of the smell of salt and marsh; of the tranquil stretch of water, at the edge of which sandpipers performed their intricate minuets; aware, too, of houses far beyond where land bent inward and where a cluster of gulls now lighted.

The air was sweet and chilly and he had left his office to walk for a time with his dog and to think of some of his problems. He did not think of his grief; it had been with him for a long time; it rose when he did and it went to bed with him; it had become part of his pattern of living. He did not think of his relationship with his sister, Sophie; that had ceased to be a problem and had, like his sorrow, become part of a pattern.

Instead, he thought of his patients – and particularly of two. Again a pattern, but not personal, although one of them had long been his friend. He thought he was learning to be involved only professionally. This had not always been so. But he believed that, if one is to do as good a job as possible, he must set aside his emotions – for emotions are untrustworthy

– and apply himself objectively.

He thought: I'll call Roger Banning in on Pete Jarvis; he's a sound man and no matter what Pete says, I must have a second opinion. He thought further: I am not equipped to deal with Mary Karlin, except in a rudimentary way. Her case requires more than kindergarten knowledge; expert advice is vital. The Karlins will go into a spin if I suggest a psychiatrist. Besides they can't afford that kind of money and there's no clinic nearby.

Somehow he must make Mary's parents see the danger. It would require infinite tact, and there are times when one tires of being tactful. There was a good man connected with the hospital. He thought: If the Karlins consent . . . It beats me how people can be so blind – so you ignore the difficulty and it goes away. I'll tell Dr. Marod frankly of their situation.

The Labrador, standing in water up to his haunches, barked at a low-flying gull, which couldn't have cared less.

Jonathan whistled and the big, black dog came out of the water, shook himself and ran toward the man. His deity had summoned. He was owned by the deity, but also, in this give-and-take relationship, he owned his god.

"Supper, Baffin," Jonathan reminded him and put his hand on the massive head. "Shake yourself again. Sophie isn't going to like this."

The Labrador shook himself. He did not feel wet because his double coat protected him; but he was obedient, since obedience was usually rational.

The dusk was deepening to darkness as they went toward the house together, over sand, through tall grass, salty and sharp, over the marshy places and into a field. The house was bright with lamplight. It was a long low structure and fitted into the landscape as if it had grown there, having been a part of it for over a century. There'd been only one addition to it in recent years – the office – one-storied and with a separate entrance.

Jonathan and his sister had known this house since they were children, their father having bought it for summer holidays. For more than thirty years the natives of this town and those bordering it had accepted the Condits. They'd ceased to be thought of as summer residents even before Jonathan and Sophie came to live, year round, four years ago.

Jonathan went into the house, the Labrador following, and Sophie came out into the square hall, stepping lightly on the wide, old boards which Mrs. Parker, the housekeeper, kept shining. "Where have you been?" she asked, although she knew well enough and added, "It's

13

past dinner time and the phone's been ringing incessantly."

"Walking," Jonathan answered, as he took off his heavy jacket, and inquired, "Anything urgent?"

"I don't think so."

He picked up the message pad from the hall table, glanced at the notations in Sophie's small, legible handwriting, and said, "I'll call back."

"Dinner –" Sophie began, but he was already sitting down and drawing the telephone toward him. He was tall, even when he sat, and a little stooped.

She spoke to the Labrador, "Don't you ever stay out of the water, Baffin?" she asked. "Go into the kitchen."

Baffin regarded her with sagacious, deep-set eyes. He knew she'd consider him wet whatever he might think. During summer in the long evening light he'd be sent outdoors. It would be summer soon enough and Baffin was not fond of heat.

He wagged his tail in a courteous gesture and padded off toward the kitchen where Mrs. Parker kept a large towel especially for him.

Contrary to tradition, Mrs. Parker was an indifferent cook, but her housekeeping was dedicated. Reticent, loyal, and shrewd, she and Baffin had much in common. Mrs. Parker endured and respected Sophie Condit and was devoted to Jonathan. She'd known them both for years, ever since, as Ann Hayes, prior to her disastrous marriage, she'd worked summers for the Condits. She had learned to open and close the house for them — this house — and to make herself part of the holiday household, a little awed by the head of the family and his reputation as a great man in his field, entranced as was everyone by his wife, and accepting the children. Mrs. Parker wasn't much older than Sophie. Nowadays she often found it difficult to reconcile her memory of Jonathan, a lanky, mischievous, outgoing boy, with the man he'd become. But Sophie hadn't changed; she still seemed to be the girl Mrs. Parker had known years ago — grown taller and older, but still determined, dominating, and keeping herself to herself.

Presently they went in to dinner, and Baffin, emerging from the kitchen, established himself beneath the arch of the doorway to the hall. Sophie would not have him in the dining room and she did not approve of the post he had selected as second choice. She remarked, "Someday when the telephone rings and I'm at the table, I'll run to answer it and fall over that great animal."

"He always manages to remove himself from

15

the path in time," her brother said mildly.

"I won't count on it. . . . Did you say you were going out?"

He was, and she knew it, but her idea of family mealtime conversation consisted mainly of asking questions to which she knew the answers.

"I promised Pete Jarvis I'd run over."

"I'd planned to go to the Guild meeting."

This meant: What if there are calls and you don't get back for office hours before Mrs. Parker leaves?

"Go ahead," said Jonathan.

"Any really enterprising town has an answering service."

"I won't be half an hour," Jonathan assured her.

Baffin was asleep. He huffed, now and then, dreaming of important matters — wings far above him, silver fins below, and also of earlier days when there'd been time for the deity to take him fishing off the town wharf, for instance, or in the boat which hadn't been in use half a dozen times last season.

"Why don't you sell it?" Sophie often demanded. "You're hardly ever in it and the money it costs, the upkeep . . ." to which Jonathan always replied, patiently, "If I sell it, I won't be able to use it if ever there's a chance."

Now Sophie said, "Jonathan . . . ?" and hesitated. He regarded her in some astonishment as she was not given to hesitation. Then she said, "I had a letter from Frances today."

It sometimes amused her brother to be willful. He asked, "Frances who?"

"How many Franceses do you know?"

"Half a dozen."

"But not six who'd write me. Frances Lawson, of course."

"So?"

She asked, exasperated, "Is that all you have to say?"

"Yes. Or is her news world-shaking? I'm waiting," Jonathan said. She did not see him wink in Baffin's direction; nor, being asleep, did Baffin.

"The Lawsons are coming down earlier than usual," Sophie said, "actually in a couple of weeks. Frances' mother hasn't been well."

Jonathan's gray eyes were amused. He said, "There's nothing wrong with Maida Lawson that a great deal less money, considerably more useful activity, and a whale of a lot of self-discipline wouldn't cure. Which, since I'm not her physician, is a nonprofessional opinion, hence not unethical."

"You could be her doctor when she's here."

"Which isn't often. It would be a waste of my

17

time and her money. Her regular man in the city can provide her with sleeping pills and tell her, no, she doesn't really drink too much; and anyone can hold her hand and sympathize with her, including you, her daughter, and the week-end guests."

"But, Jonathan —"

"Oh, for heaven's sake!" he said. "I had a bellyful of that sort of practice in New York — delinquent debutantes, desperate dowagers and devastating divorcées."

"I suppose by that last crack you mean Frances?"

"Check."

Sophie rang the bell and Mrs. Parker clumped into the room, lean and unsmiling, to clear away and then bring dessert which tonight was a species of Indian pudding.

After Mrs. Parker had returned to the kitchen, Sophie commented, "Her cooking gets worse every year."

"But she grows better," said Jonathan. "It's merely that she doesn't like to cook; it doesn't interest her; it's simply part of the job, so she does it. What would we do without her?"

He recognized his error a fraction too late. This was an excuse for Sophie to say, "Well, of course, you insisted on burying yourself in this godforsaken place where you can't get really efficient help. . . ."

So she said it and he shook his head and answered, "It's strange, but I don't feel buried." The mischief Mrs. Parker would have recognized glinted briefly in his eyes, and he added, "You were always a good cook, Sophie."

She asked shortly, "And when would I have time?"

As a matter of sober fact Sophie like Seascape. There was the Guild and the Rector, Henry Stiles, a widower; also the painters and writers, resident or transient, and the ruling social arbiters. A number of people amused or stimulated her; a few, she liked. In summer, Seascape came alive with cottagers and tourists, who were, generally speaking, to be deplored, but useful for conversational purposes. In summer, Jonathan's practice was incredible because he was the only general practitioner in easy reach of several towns, all of which also burgeoned in summer.

Jonathan, contemplating summer, usually thought and sometimes said: Accidents, half-drownings, poison ivy, clamshell cuts, firecrackers, gastric upsets, viruses, emergencies.

Mrs. Parker brought coffee and Sophie poured it into the big, old cups. Here Mrs. Parker excelled; she made wonderful coffee and equally good tea. But then, as Jonathan had

19

once explained to his sister, "Mrs. Parker likes coffee and tea; she is bored with food."

Baffin woke and followed Mrs. Parker through the kitchen door. He was thirsty, having been running in his dreams. He'd avoided the vicinity of the dining table, not even pausing to speak to Jonathan.

"He smells of clam mud," Sophie said.

"One characteristic of the breed," Jonathan told her, "is that they don't smell."

"You and your fool dog!"

He drank his coffee and enjoyed it. He felt relaxed. The little walk had done him good. He'd tell Pete tonight that he had decided upon a consultant. Pete wouldn't like it and his wife, Susan, would back him up. But he has to see it my way, Jonathan thought – hospital, tests, observation, the works. He'd suggested all this before. Pete wasn't having any. But he'd have to now. I'll tell him, Jonathan thought, that unless he follows orders I can't be responsible.

And tomorrow he'd talk carefully to Mary Karlin's frightened, stubborn, willfully blind parents. . . . Responsibility was one of the burdens.

He thought, not for the first time: How much I knew as an intern, as a resident, and in the Navy – and, of course, as assistant to his medical holiness in the city – and how little I

20

know now when too many depend upon me.

It sets you apart from other men, the knowledge you once soaked up like a blotter, the eagerness born of what you thought you knew, and then the growing, deepening awareness that you didn't know as much as you'd believed and that, no matter how much you came to know, it would never be enough.

He rose, and Sophie with him; she was a tall woman, but he topped her by a head. She was fair and he dark; there was a little gray in his hair and none in hers, although she was his senior by several years.

She said abruptly, "You know, of course, that Frances Lawson is coming back here this summer because of you."

It was a statement, not a question. He said irritably, going into the hall, opening the closet door, "I don't know anything of the kind, Sophie. The Lawsons invade Seascape every summer — except when they're somewhere else."

"She had intended to go abroad this year," Sophie said.

"So she changed her mind," said Jonathan, putting on his jacket.

He turned toward the door to the passageway and Sophie asked, "Now, where are you going?"

"Just to get my bag," he said. "It's routine."

There were times when Sophie, who loved her brother in her fashion, disliked him intensely. This evening was one of them.

She followed him through the passageway to the office. They could hear Mrs. Parker singing high and tunelessly in the kitchen, and Baffin bumbling around.

"If only you'd admit which side your bread's buttered on —" she began.

"I do. The wrong side. It always falls on the rug. And now I'm in something of a hurry," Jonathan reminded her.

She watched him go outside, through the office door, heard him whistle, saw the Labrador bounce out of the kitchen and heard the car start.

One of Sophie's friends, a schoolteacher who spent her summers in Seascape, had said to her not long since, "How can you immolate yourself this way? Jonathan's a good man and a fine doctor, but how do you stand it? I stay here only because my aunt left me the house, and I haven't yet found a good buyer."

And Sophie had replied, "But I like Seascape and I'm needed."

Tonight, however, she didn't feel needed; she felt nothing but discontent. She stood at the hall table and telephoned her closest friend in the Guild, Alice Winsor.

"Alice?" she said. "Sophie here."

This was a trick she'd picked up at the time her father had sent her to England, after her mother's death a long time ago. It had been the older Doctor Condit's prescription for the sort of cardiac difficulty not in general medical books but often encountered in novels. What else can you do for an efficient graduate nurse who does what many have done before her (and will, after she's dust), which is to fall in love with a married man who, whatever his personal reaction, had no intention of sacrificing a splendid surgical career to say nothing of his wife's money.

"I'm sorry," Sophie told her friend, "I've a raging headache. I won't be at the meeting, Alice."

She hung up and went upstairs. Her mother's little sitting room now housed the television set. Sophie sat down and looked at its empty face.

When Seascape's Doctor Lacy had died and Jonathan suggested buying the practice from his widow, with part of the legacy his father had left him, Sophie had humored him. She'd had to. She couldn't permit him to go away alone. If Jonathan's wife had lived, he probably would have continued as assistant to Holsworthy, and eventually inherited that solid practice. But Edna hadn't lived.

In some ways Edna had been like herself; that is to say, an efficient nurse, attractive, and romantically dedicated to one man. (But I got over that long ago, Sophie thought.) But Edna hadn't been right for Jonathan . . . too young . . . and not ambitious. Whatever he might have made of himself, it wouldn't have been Edna's doing; she would have been content to walk in whatever path he selected, including the present one. She'd never have pushed him.

Frances Lawson would push; and she had everything to push with.

Sophie sighed. I was better off at the hospital, she thought. People, excitement, the satisfaction of seeing things done. For some years before, and during Jonathan's marriage, she'd held an executive position at Lister Memorial.

"What am I doing here?" she asked herself.

For the last few years she'd believed that she was, in addition to making Jonathan comfortable and running his office – appointments, bills, telephones – on her way to another executive job via Henry Stiles. As his wife she would have her own house to order (this one was only half hers), and Henry's children to look after. She could manage the young people well enough; it only took firmness, measured sympathy, and understanding – and she could still keep an eye on her brother. Mrs. Parker would stay on with Jonathan until she dropped and there were elderly nurses in the district who'd jump at an office job.

Sophie hadn't reckoned with competition . . . and Dr. Stiles's temperament. A clergyman is as much pursued as is a doctor, married or unmarried. Henry Stiles, a widower for some years, exhibited no sign of desiring to alter his status. He was a gentle, charming man and, as his women parishioners said over the teacups, "so marvelously spiritual." Perhaps he should not have married the first time; possibly he was that rarest of men, a born celibate. But he'd not ignored St. Paul's injunction. Maybe he hadn't been seriously burned, but indubitably he'd married and fathered a boy – now at college – and a girl in high school.

Yet, Sophie thought, he required someone who would be devoted to him – as devoted as the first Mrs. Stiles, but with more verve – who would take active interest and part in the parish, surround him with comfort and comprehension, and infect him with ambition. For there are Bishops.

She switched on the television set, not bothering to alter the channel and sat down to watch, without pleasure. The telephone rang and she went into Jonathan's rather austere bedroom to answer it. The windows were open and the white curtains blew straight in the wind. Sophie spoke, listened, wrote down the message and then stood a moment at the bedside table. The lamp was lighted and she picked up Edna's photograph and looked at it — the young face, the vulnerable mouth, the wide-spaced eyes. She felt no grief; she had never felt grief, only concern for Jonathan.

What had he seen in Edna? What did he still see? Was he still blaming himself for her fatal accident? That was nonsense. It hadn't been his fault. His sister had told him that over and over.

She went back to the little sitting room. If nothing interesting developed on the screen, she'd read, listen for the phone and for Jonathan's car returning.

His evening office hours were restricted to a few patients who couldn't come during the day, and it was tacitly understood that Sophie need not be in the waiting room.

A long evening stretched out before her.

Chapter Two

Pete Jarvis lived on the top of an uphill country road and from the old small windows of his old small house he and his wife Susan could see for miles; an enviable view of sand dunes and water.

"Well," Jonathan told Baffin, "wish me luck, I need it. Want to run a little?"

Baffin allowed that was a good idea.

Jonathan got out and Baffin followed by the simple expedient of leaping over the front seat. He knew the door would be left open for his return and Jonathan knew that, whatever delectable smells might tempt the Labrador, he would not go far afield or be seduced into exploring the cliff road beneath this one.

Jonathan went up the path which was bordered with whitewashed stones, but before he could knock Susan had the door open.

"Heard the car," she explained. "Come in, Doctor."

He took her hand, smiling. She had always

called him Jon until he came to Seascape to practice. He had known this little house a long time; Susan had made sandwiches for him here when, in other days, Peter had taken a young boy fishing.

"Baffin outside?" Susan asked. "You want he should come in?"

"He's having a run, thanks, Susan. Where's Pete?"

"In the kitchen."

The kitchen was bigger than the parlor and it was lived in. Pete had his favorite chair there, broken down and comfortable to his contours. He had his feet on a stool and was reading a newspaper with his glasses half way down his beaky nose.

Pete looked up, "Ben Casey," he remarked, "wrong night."

The Jarvises had a television set. It, too, was in the kitchen. Some of the trawler captains had given it to Pete when he'd retired and sold the *"Susan J."*

"Why aren't you watching the pretty pictures?" Jonathan asked.

"Mostly agabble, now . . . take them news-boys, the ones who explain everything to you like you was six years old. They think they're God A'mighty. Take Jon's coat, Susan."

She took it, remarking that he'd need it

tonight, the wind was rising and sharp. And Jonathan thought how much Pete and his wife looked alike; small, thin, wiry, with bright blue eyes and weathered brown skins. But they'd lived together for fifty years and people often tend to look alike after that long. They were alone. There'd been a child once, but it had died in infancy. As far as Jonathan knew there were no relatives closer than a niece of Susan's who lived in another state.

"Sit down," said Peter, "or you aimin' to prod or somethin'?"

"Not tonight," said Jonathan, taking a straight chair by the kitchen table. "How do you feel, Pete?"

His patient considered and then reached a conclusion. "I've felt better," he said, "and worse. I didn't expect you."

"Why not? I said I'd drop by one evening."

Susan brought him coffee in a chipped, willow-ware cup. It was black and as strong as a new dictator.

"No, no sugar, thanks, nor condensed milk."

"Seems this is a social call," Pete remarked, "so see that you don't charge me." He grinned. He had very few teeth and Jonathan had never been able to persuade him that his digestion would be improved if he remedied the lack.

"This visit is for free. I've come to ask a favor."

Pete slanted a wary eye. He had excellent sight — the far-seeing, patient sight of the fisherman he'd been until last autumn.

"What kind?"

"I want you in the hospital for tests with Dr. Banning as consultant."

"What does he know that you don't?"

"Thanks. Perhaps I just want him to confirm that I know something."

"About me?"

"Yes, but, generally speaking, about medicine."

"I hate hospitals," Pete said. He hadn't been in one as a patient since the end of the First World War. "Costs like hell, too, these days."

Jonathan said lightly, "You have hospitalization. Why not get your money's worth? You want to die without ever having used it?"

"Got a point there," Pete agreed. "Susan," he suggested mildly, "suppose you clear out."

Susan did so.

"Now then," said Pete, "you think I got cancer?"

He looked at his friend and then away; a thoughtful look, unclouded. Jonathan had the impression that Pete Jarvis had looked

30

so often, and for so long, at far horizons that he wasn't afraid of this one.

"I don't know," he said honestly, "but we must find out."

"So what if I have?" Pete inquired. "No law against a man's dying in his own bed without all the pokin' and pryin', is there?"

"None," Jonathan admitted, "if that's the way you'd want it."

"That's the way."

"And is it the way Susan would want it?"

"If I say so."

"Susan," said Jonathan, "has a mind of her own."

"That's right," said Pete, "when I give in to her."

"Well," Jonathan said, after a minute, "it's up to you. I can order you into the hospital and if you refuse, wash my hands of you. Or I can wait until you're too flat out to know what's happening, shove you in an ambulance, and see to it that Susan signs you in. On the other hand, you may not have cancer, Pete, in which case we – Dr. Banning and I – will recommend treatment we believe will help you. You can't tell me – not that I'd put it past you – that you enjoyed that last attack."

"It was hell," Pete said simply. He laughed and cleared his throat. Then he said, his face grave, his eyes amused, "Something I et no doubt."

"Could be," said Jonathan, "knowing your passion for Eyobang pie."

"Had chowder tonight; you should've come along earlier. Some left, I guess. Want for Susan to heat it up for you?"

"No thanks. Look, Pete. Let's get down to cases — your case. I'm supposed to be your doctor . . . No one else would take what I've taken from you. I daresay I'll have to anesthetize poor Banning — but, quite seriously, I can't be responsible for you, or to Susan, unless you'll consent to the tests and a second opinion. You aren't being fair to me, Pete, to say nothing of yourself and Susan."

"O.K., O.K., but it's a waste of time and money."

"Not money. You have it made, remember?"

"All right, dammit!"

Jonathan drew a long breath and set down his cup and then Pete said, "Maybe I don't want to know. To tell the truth, Jon, I'm scared."

"Not you. I don't believe it."

"Oh, not for me," said Pete. "Been a little dull since I quit fishin'. For Susan." He paused and then grinned again. "All them pretty girls at the hospital. Went to see Sam Locke there, year or two back — remember him? — he owned the *Betty Belle*. Make a man blush the way girls skipped in and out of that room and Sam next to nekkid."

Jonathan rose and walked over to Pete's dilapidated easy chair. He thought: He's lost weight since I saw him just a few days ago. He put his hand on the thin shoulder and said, "Thanks. I'll make the arrangements tomorrow and let you know."

"Damned if you don't sound like Phineas," said Pete. Phineas Grey was the Seascape undertaker. "Don't go yet. Been savin' a story for you."

It was a good story, bawdy, funny, replete with local color and unfortunately for its protagonists, true. After that, Pete wanted to talk about clamming. He'd done his share in his day. And clamming always brought up the summer idiots who ruined the ground and left pitfalls for the unwary beachcomber or bather.

Presently Jonathan left and Susan was waiting for him by the front door. Her hands were locked together beneath her apron so that, he suspected, he would not see them shaking.

"How bad is he?" she whispered.

"He's sick, Susan, and getting sicker. But he's promised to go into the hospital . . . After the tests, we'll know more."

She said dully, "I don't need tests to tell me

33

he's bad. He don't eat — and he don't sleep much. He hurts."

Jonathan touched her shoulder, so like Pete's, hard and thin. He said gently, "I'll do all I can. . . . Is there someone who'd stay with you while he's away for three or four days?"

Susan said, "I can stay near the hospital. I've a friend who'd let me have a room."

Pete was roaring from the kitchen, "Susan, come back here. Jon's got better things to do than stand there gabbin' with you all night. Besides, the door's open, like to blow me out of my chair and you'll catch your death of cold."

Jonathan said good night and went out. The wind was cold, but he was sweating.

Baffin was waiting in the car on the back seat. Jonathan got in and reached over to touch him as if for reassurance.

He drove home thinking: Too late? But I tried; I've tried for weeks. Maybe even last month it would have been too late.

He hated to put his old friend through — what was it Pete had said? — the poking and the prying and the prodding; perhaps surgery. But unless you poked and pried and prodded, you wouldn't know — not actually.

Think of something else. Think of Elsie Watson for whom it had not been too late; think of the people last winter. Asian flu, virus

34

pneumonia, other emergencies . . . the Bailey kid with the measles, plus complications – and all of them walking around now, good as new.

When he reached home, two cars were parked there with no one in them. Presumably the patients were in the waiting room. He didn't lock the office when he went out evenings on call. He kept only the narcotics under lock and key.

More upstairs lights than usual. Perhaps Sophie hadn't gone to her meeting after all.

He took Baffin into the kitchen, thinking of his sister and Henry Stiles. She'd better give up, he concluded. Henry, for all his gentle manner and shy charm, was not a man to be pushed into anything, especially matrimony. He was Jonathan's patient and as stubborn in his own way as Pete Jarvis.

Don't think of Pete. You know damned well he's scared and not of pretty girls; not of dying, either; but of leaving Susan alone.

Sooner or later everyone's left alone.

He thought: I'm scared, too – for Pete – and went into his office.

Something more than an hour later he turned off the lights, called Baffin, and went into the living room to switch the lamps off there before going upstairs. He was tired, though it had not been a hard day, not nearly as hard as most.

Emotionally tired, he thought grimly. Forget it. Forget that you've known Pete since you were no higher than a bulrush; forget the times he took you fishing; forget Susan and what you've been seeing in her eyes these past few weeks.

These are the things you must get used to and expect; and, also, accept. Every time you thought you were used to them you found you weren't.

He thought wryly: Sophie would have made a better doctor . . . cool, calm, objective.

"So I try," he told himself. "Yet against my considered judgment, I still become involved."

Edna . . . She'd been young, earnest, and understanding. If she'd lived, perhaps she would have grown tired of the schedule, the uncertain meals, the night calls — for his holiness, Holsworthy, would not take night calls as long as he had a willing, able, eager-beaver assistant. You don't know what people will grow up into . . . he'd never know about Edna now. But as long as they had been together, she'd understood.

Water over the dam. Blood on the brownstone steps. Edna running out to call him to the telephone, that winter night, and slipping on the glaze of ice. . . .

As he reached his room, Sophie came out of

hers. She was, as the saying goes, a fine figure of a woman, even though Henry Stiles didn't appear to appreciate the fact. Her hair, which was long, was braided. She had on a dressing gown and there was a book in her hands.

He said, "I didn't wake you, did I?"

"No, I was reading; and it isn't late. I let Mrs. Somers and the Fawcett boy in to wait for you."

"Thanks. I thought you were going out."

"I had a headache," said Sophie. She added, "I took some calls, nothing urgent; I made some appointments for you, too . . . everything's written down. How was Pete Jarvis?"

"Not good," – Jonathan sighed and straightened his shoulders – "but at least I've persuaded him to go in for observation."

"Was it difficult?"

"Not as tough as I thought it would be."

Sometimes he talked with her of his cases – she was not only his sister but a nurse – but this was not one of the times.

"Well," she said, "you're doing all you can. Good night, Jonathan."

"Good night."

Now he was in his room, the door was shut and Baffin was looking at an empty water bowl. Jonathan went into the adjoining bath and refilled the bowl. He looked at himself in the mirror. "You look older than Pete," he said aloud.

Baffin barked and Jonathan brought him the water. He didn't drink it, just smiled slightly and went to bed.

The room smelled of sea and salt, and there was the sound of the sea in it and the wind. All the rooms were like that, open to sun and wind and sea. Jonathan thought of his mother who had done a little rebuilding to her liking. There was privacy here, and comfort. . . .

It was a bigger house than he and Sophie needed. Four bedrooms upstairs, two baths. And downstairs, also a bedroom and bath in case, as had once been the pattern, the cook lived in. The kitchen had twice been modernized, once by Mrs. Condit, once by her daughter, Sophie.

Edna had loved this house. He'd brought her here before they were married, during the last summer of his father's life. She would have liked living here. There might have been children clattering over the wide boards, or running barefoot on the beach . . . But perhaps he would not have come to Seascape if Edna had lived. Perhaps he would have gone on with Holsworthy. . . .

He'd met Edna before he went into the service. That is, he'd noticed her as a student nurse. He'd been resident then, ending his rotating service. Then, when he came back and Holsworthy offered him the job, he'd seen her again. She'd graduated in the meantime and was in charge of one of the floors, women's surgical.

He'd fallen in love suddenly, which was something he had never expected to do. She said she'd been in love with him always.

"Always?"

"Well, ever since I went into training and that seems like always."

They hadn't come here on their brief wedding trip. They'd been married in the autumn by Edna's father in the small town in which she'd been born and had gone South for a few days. He was glad now that she had been here only once for a summer weekend. She'd had the guest room down the hall, so that, except for her picture, this room had nothing of her in it. The walls were painted a cool, pale green. There was one etching and two water colors on them. The etching had been his father's; the water colors he'd bought after coming here to live. There were bookshelves, and the necessary furniture, including Baffin's bed, but no more.

Jonathan undressed, took a book at random from a shelf, and got into bed. Baffin said something. He might have been asking: Are you all right?

Jonathan picked up the messages Sophie had left for him. He knew the names – the chronic asthmatic, the little girl whose arm he'd set. Methodical Sophie would have entered all appointments on his office desk pad. . . . At the end of the message list Sophie had written, "Frances Lawson telephoned. She'll be at the Inn alone for the weekend and hopes to see you. Says it's important."

"Hell," said Jonathan, and Baffin grunted.

He dropped the message pad on the bedside table and wondered what Frances was up to now. He'd known her slightly during the first summer of his Seascape practice . . . she had come as an impatient patient, obviously annoyed at having to wait her turn. He'd forgotten her difficulty – poison ivy, clamshell cut, a summer cold? Toward the summer's end, Sophie had met Frances at an art exhibition and the first thing Jonathan knew he was dining at the Lawsons' mammoth, quite lovely house, "Driftwood," in one of the newer sections. He'd been called away before dinner was over and had returned later to have a mild Scotch and soda and take Sophie home.

The following summer Frances had been in Switzerland, but her parents had come to Seascape; Mrs. Lawson with her retinue of male and female hangers-on and Mr. Lawson for weekends.

But Frances had taken a fancy to Jonathan; she'd made it plain enough in a way that might be termed both casual and practiced.

One of the lesser rewards of the practice of medicine is that, when you don't want to go somewhere or meet someone, you have a ready, plausible excuse . . . ninety per cent of the time valid.

Frances Lawson — she had resumed her maiden name after her divorce — was one of the prettiest women he'd ever seen and he was no less susceptible to appearances than any other man. But shadow is not substance.

He tossed aside the book he hadn't been reading, turned off the light, and went to sleep.

Chapter Three

At breakfast next morning, he asked, "Did Frances indicate what she wants of me?"

"No. . . . I asked her to dinner, but she refused."

"I'm not astonished; she's had dinner here before. As for seeing me, I have office hours."

"I don't think it's on a professional basis," Sophie said blandly.

Jonathan shrugged. He said, "All summer's ahead; you can haunt Driftwood and Frances can come here whenever she fancies plain living. . . ."

He didn't add: it's half your house and if you want to encourage the woman and set your matrimonial traps — that made him smile, with his eyes — it's up to you.

"Aren't you curious to know why she suddenly decided to come to the Inn?"

"Frankly, yes," Jonathan admitted, and this time he smiled openly. Sophie relaxed; her own curiosity was bad for her blood pressure.

Jonathan had a busy day — house calls, the arrangements to make for Pete Jarvis. He did not return for lunch, but called Sophie from the hospital. On his way home he stopped at the Karlins'.

Sam Karlin was part owner of a hardware store. Jonathan had called him there to ask if he could take time out to come home and see him in, say, half an hour. He knew that Mary would be at school.

Presently he sat in a forbidding, orderly parlor and talked to the Karlins about their daughter. She'd been his patient for some time. She had a history of bad headaches, of what her mother termed bilious attacks, and also of what she called tantrums.

Mary's school work was erratic. She was quiet and withdrawn most of the time. She did not make friends. She liked to be by herself.

She was, her mother said, in great demand as a baby sitter because there was nothing flighty about her and no boy friends to complicate matters.

After a few minutes' fencing, Jonathan said, "I'm sorry to have called you away from the store, Mr. Karlin, but I wanted to see you both when Mary wasn't here. I've reason to believe she's emotionally disturbed and I'd like Dr. Marod to see her."

Mrs. Karlin asked, flushing, "Isn't he the psychiatrist?"

"That's right."

Sam Karlin protested, "Now don't go barking up the wrong tree, Doc. There's nothing the matter with Mary except headaches and you can't blame her for getting upset when she has them — at her age."

"She's sixteen," Jonathan said, "and has had all the tests I can give her to determine the cause of the headaches. Her eyes are all right; we know she hasn't a brain tumor; and the allergy tests failed to turn up anything which would account for the recurrent condition. I strongly recommend that Dr. Marod see her; he may be able to help her."

"But you've talked to her," Mrs. Karlin said.

"Unfortunately only *at* her," Jonathan answered. "She's never opened up to me."

Karlin shook his head. "I don't hold with psychiatrists," he said, "and, anyway, we can't afford it."

"I'll explain the situation to Dr. Marod —" Jonathan began.

"But there's no need," Mrs. Karlin interrupted. "Thousands of people have headaches. You make it sound like she's" — she swallowed hard — "crazy, or something."

"I'm sorry I gave that impression," Jonathan said.

He rose; there was nothing he could do here. Karlin said, "Well, it's good of you to be bothered, but you needn't be. . . . She'll outgrow this, Doc. . . . Seems like nowadays people are always looking for trouble that isn't there."

Driving home he thought: One of the failures. And not his fault. He could only pray — and that was true enough; he prayed without words, almost without consciousness of praying, very often — that he was wrong and Mary Karlin's parents right. But he was pretty sure he wasn't wrong.

When he reached his house there were cars parked there, among them a car he recognized, a fast, underslung foreign car, canary yellow. Frances Lawson's.

He went directly into the office where there were patients waiting and Sophie said, "You're late."

"Not very."

"Frances is here," she informed him.

"I know. I saw the car." He sat down at his desk and then looked up, unaware of how the Karlin case (closed, he thought) showed in his face, the weariness, the heavier lines. "I'll be busy for a couple of

45

hours," he said. "Tell her I'm sorry."

"She's gone walking with Baffin," Sophie reported to his astonishment, "but they'll be back. We'll have some tea . . . Come in when you can."

He put in something over two hours, concentrating on problems, new or old, trying to erase from his mind every thought except the immediate.

When he went into the living room Frances said, "Well, finally. How are you, Jon?"

"Fine." He shook hands with her, smiling. Small, and — what was the word? — vibrant, with ash-blond hair, a flawless skin and delicate features dominated by eyes which were startling, being unexpectedly brown. She was, as always, beautifully made up, but he conceded to himself that even with her face washed clean she'd be lovely.

Sophie poured him a cup of tea and offered him some little cakes (not Mrs. Parker's) at which he shook his head and the conversation drifted along: the summer to come, the people they mutually knew, the elder Lawsons, the past season in the city and then Sophie said, "Well, I've some things to do in the office. I run out on Jonathan now and then, you know," she told Frances. "He has to make his own appointments, take his own calls and temporarily keep his own books."

46

"He looks capable enough," said Frances in her light, hurrying voice. "You spoil him, Sophie."

When they were alone, he asked, "What did you want to see me about?"

"The hospital."

He raised an eyebrow at her. "Thinking of surgery as a summer diversion?"

"Oh, don't be so stuffy," she said. "You are most of the time. I want to know — can they use a volunteer?"

"They can always use volunteers." He looked at her startled. "Not you?" he said, incredulous.

"Listen, Buster," said Frances, "I've worked my head off since last autumn in a hospital four times the size of yours."

"What doing, exactly?"

She told him, whatever was needed; most recently she had been assigned to the children's wards. "I'm good with children," she added with infuriating smugness, "and don't say it . . ."

"What was I going to say?"

"That you wouldn't have thought it."

"That's right," Jonathan admitted.

"Well, give me a recommendation or something," she said carelessly, and rose. "We'll be coming up for good before Memorial Day. And tell Sophie I'm sorry — I'd go to the office and tell her myself, but I have to run. I have a date."

He didn't doubt it. Who was the year-round artist with whom she'd been seen so much last summer? Kim – Kim something? Sylvester, that was it. Kim Sylvester.

He went upstairs for a jacket and returned to whistle for Baffin. The yellow car was gone; Sophie was still in the office, for, he thought, no very good reason. Baffin, who was communing with Mrs. Parker, emerged and slowly followed Jonathan down to the beach.

"Bushed, are you?" asked Jonathan. "She must have set a fast pace," and added to himself: That figures.

He thought of Frances Lawson at the hospital and shuddered; she could if she'd a mind to – and he suspected she had – raise considerable havoc among the males who functioned there in any capacity and from the ages eight to ninety.

That, however, would be no skin off his nose, he informed himself, and unless it got her into mischief, it would keep her out of it, which was, he decided, a rather remarkable prognosis.

He wondered if he liked Frances Lawson. He didn't dislike her, and there were times when she amused him, but not as often as she irritated him. However, he liked to look at her.

"Steady," he said aloud and Baffin, for once trotting soberly beside him, looked up

48

wounded. A steadier gentleman never lived. "I don't mean you," Jonathan soothed him.

Any man who falls to recognize interest — a nice way of putting it — in a woman's regard is either an idiot or incredibly naïve. Jonathan was neither.

Since Edna's death — a few encounters — casual, releasing, brief, and no illusions. . . .

He was not, by nature, celibate. However, his profession gave him very little time for fun and games . . . not that other men, also of his profession, hadn't found the time. Perhaps, he thought, walking back to the house, that's one reason why I came to Seascape.

Practicing in a big impersonal city was different. Seascape was small and well informed at all times. Of course a doctor had to watch his step wherever he was; but in Seascape every step was noted and measured.

Now and again at rare intervals he went to the city for a brief holiday. Sometimes Sophie went, too. They stayed at a small hotel and no one questioned what he saw or did there . . . except Sophie, who after the first time, had learned to keep quiet. A rarity for her, but Jonathan lost his temper so seldom that when he did, it was terrifying.

Pete Jarvis grumbled his way into the hospital, met Jonathan's confrere, Doctor Banning, with courteous reluctance and submitted to various tests. On the day before he was to complete them he died – suddenly and quietly.

"But," said Banning to Jonathan, dismayed, "he had a routine EKG, as you know. His heart seemed perfectly sound – and then this. . . . Well, it's spared him a lot of suffering."

Jonathan knew that, too. He'd seen all the reports so far; he'd made a point of stopping by to see Pete briefly every day. Susan had been there as much as possible.

Jonathan, sitting with her that evening after the funeral arrangements had been made, wondered what he could say to her, beyond the helpless routine: "We couldn't have forseen it, Susan . . . I'd give my right hand if –"

She broke in, her small face frozen. "I know," she said. And then, "He didn't want to go to the hospital."

It was a tacit reproach, to which he could only reply, "I know. But it would have happened anyway."

"Mebbe so," said Susan dully, "and mebbe not."

After a minute she said, "Olive – that's my niece – is coming to stay awhile. Perhaps she can get a summer job. She's been teaching, but things aren't good at home, and her contract runs out, so she thought maybe she might get a

50

teaching job here in the fall. She has to go home after the" — she swallowed and he saw the thin, hard cords on her neck working — "funeral, but she'll come back when school's out."

Jonathan nodded, relieved that someone would be in the little house with Pete's wife. "If there's anything I can do . . ." he began.

"Nothing," said Susan. "We had a little saved. I can go out to work. Olive will pay board . . . This isn't sudden," she added. "I had a letter from her before . . . I talked to her on the phone since."

Jonathan came home from the funeral in a towering rage — at himself, at his profession, and at the finality of what he had just witnessed. There were a great many people, he knew, who did not believe death was finality. Sometimes he didn't himself. Today he did.

He had seen the niece with Susan, a slight young woman with remarkable composure.

Sophie had gone to the services, too, in the church and at the cemetery. Driving home she said something which he answered shortly, and she remarked, "You needn't bite my head off."

"Sorry."

She said after a moment, "You've had quite a few years to get used to situations like this, Jonathan."

He said savagely, "I'll never get used to them. When I think I have . . ." He stopped and then

51

suggested, "Let's not talk about it, Sophie."

She was quiet the rest of the way and, when they reached the house, relieved to see several parked cars. At least he'd have to put Pete's death aside and look after the living, she thought.

Susan wrote him a few days later. Olive, she said, had gone back to her folks and teaching. "She'll return soon's school's out." She added in her cramped writing, "Pete and me, we been talking it over ever since she wrote me a while back. He likes" — she'd crossed out the last word and written — "*liked* her a lot and thought it would be good for us to have some one young around. She's my youngest brother's girl," she went on, "and Pete thought she'd be company for me. Anyway, she's welcome and if she likes it here, it might work out. I talked to Sam Karlin yesterday; she can work in the hardware shop this summer and she's already written to someone about a job in the school. Home Ec. is what she teaches."

Then she said, "I think I was short with you the other night. I didn't meant to be. Pete, he thought the world of you and I do, too, Doctor. And I appreciate everything you did and tried to do."

He'd go to see Susan soon, he thought, putting the letter aside.

Memorial Day had come and gone; early summer tourists arrived and some summer residents who didn't have children in school; the big cars clogged the town streets — among them Frances Lawson's — the enormous vehicle which was her father's, and the smaller, no less impressive car which her mother drove.

Jonathan saw Frances briefly at the hospital, where she told him she'd been working for a week. The volunteer uniform became her and he thought that it was no marvel that men fell in love with nurses — probationers, graduates, aides, volunteers; the uniforms, however differing, made a plain woman attractive and a pretty woman prettier.

"Be seein' you," said Frances and went about her business. He went out into the apricot sunlight, standing a moment on the worn hospital steps. He heard a dog barking; that would be Baffin who had seen him. He thought, walking toward his car: She'll get tired of it.

A few days later he had a light office and then an emergency call from the hospital. Returning, he made a house call not far from the Jarvis house. There'd been a spectacular sunset and the afterglow was rose-gold, peach and violet. He thought: I'll stop by and see Susan. She was working, he knew, part time in one of the smaller restuarants. Approaching the house he saw the girl — what was her name? — Olive Evans, walking without haste along the road bordered with jack pine and scrub oak.

Jonathan pulled up. "How about a lift?" he asked.

Olive looked up and smiled. She was, you'd think, a plain girl, with brown hair and neat, undistinguished features, but when she smiled her face came to life. She said, "Why, thanks, Doctor Condit."

She got in and he asked, "How's your aunt? I was just about to stop by."

She answered soberly, "She's well enough, physically. She keeps busy . . . and never cries. Sometimes I hear her stirring late at night; that's all."

Baffin spoke to her from the back seat and she turned to stroke his head. She said, "I like dogs," and then added, "But Aunt Susan isn't home, Doctor. They asked her to stay on for a while this evening."

"Oh? I'm sorry. Tell her I'll stop again. And don't let her overdo — Olive — if that's all right with you," he added. "I'm pretty close to your aunt."

"Olive's fine with me . . . Yes, I'll watch her. But she has to keep going. In a way, I suppose she'd rather not. . . ."

He knew what she meant and nodded. He

54

thought: Susan's lucky to have her, she's understanding.

He stopped the car, asking, "How about the teaching job?"

Her face flashed again into animation. She said, "Isn't it wonderful? They had someone engaged, but it seems she can't come; her mother is very ill or something. So, I'm hired."

"Congratulations." He got out to open the door and said, "Goodnight. I'll see Susan — and you — soon."

He was smiling as he drove away. Nice girl. . . . How old was she? Twenty-six, twenty-eight? Sensible, serene, and — he returned again to the word — understanding.

When he reached home, there was a note from Sophie. She said she'd tried to reach him at the hospital. There was a special Guild meeting and she was going to supper with Alice Winsor first. Mrs. Parker would look after him.

This was his night off; no evening office hours — nothing unless there was an emergency.

There was still light and he decided to have a quick swim before supper. He told Mrs. Parker, who nodded, tolerantly. A few minutes later he and Baffin were swimming. The cool buoyant water felt good; the day had been unseasonably warm.

Walking back from the beach, he saw in front of the house the canary-colored car. About twenty feet long, he figured.

Frances was standing beside it, smoking. "Night off?" she asked.

"In a manner of speaking."

"Good. Take me out to dinner." Imperious, but casual.

Jonathan smiled. He said, "O.K. . . . . Suppose you go in and wait. I won't be long."

"Can I mix you a drink without Mrs. Parker falling apart?"

"You can. Scotch on the rocks. Light."

He dripped his way into the house after Frances, and on the way upstairs he thought: Why in the devil did I say I'd take her to dinner?

But he knew. He was lonely. And Frances was amusing; also, she wasn't, he informed himself, a part of reality.

Mrs. Parker, to whom he'd spoken briefly, had just shaken her head and remarked, "Stew keeps. Better next day."

Frances mixed the drinks with Mrs. Parker bringing ice and glasses and an aura of mild disapproval, and sat down to wait.

It was, she thought, futile, frustrating and stupid to be in love with Jonathan Condit. But she was; she'd gone away one summer in order

56

to distract herself and try to find someone or something else. She hadn't. He was an exasperating man. He didn't know she was alive. If I had something the matter with me, she thought wryly, he'd rush to my rescue. His bedside manner — if the office side is any indication — doesn't wear a gardenia in the buttonhole, but he'd look after me all right; he'd care whether I lived or died — the patient, not the person.

When he came downstairs, he asked, "What made you think I wouldn't be busy this evening?"

"I'm psychic," said Frances lazily. "Also, I called Sophie." She slanted her brown eyes at him. "Sophie is on my side. She allowed as how this was your free evening, provided no one suffered a ruptured appendix —"

"I rarely commit surgery —"

"Ptomaine, leprosy, a broken leg." Frances raised her glass. "I want to talk to you outside hospital corridors or office hours."

He thought, smiling: Sophie dreamed up that Guild meeting, but fast.

Baffin yawned his way to the rug beside him and Frances asked, "How are you, Mac?"

"He doesn't care to be called out of his name. . . . Where do you want to eat?"

"The Inn. It will be full of people, but I can manage a table."

He said mildly, "I thought I was taking you to dinner."

"Sorry. *You* can manage one. It's a reasonably big dining room," she added, "and the prices are reasonably small. . . . Easy on the pocketbook." She set down her glass. "So, let's go."

"I thought you wanted to talk to me."

"Over dinner, and without chaperone."

"Mrs. Parker?" He laughed. He said, "Wait till I tell her where I'll be. She said she'd stay on awhile." He rose, towering over Frances. He added, "I'll tell her we won't be late."

"Of course not," said Frances, with an exaggerated sigh.

On the way out, "We'll use my car," he said, "that is, if it doesn't offend your aesthetic sense."

"Not at all. I love slumming. But why?"

"In case I'm called. On second thought, you drive yours so if I'm called, you can get home."

"Without interrupting the practice of medicine," she murmured. "All right, Jon; you're the doctor."

Mrs. Parker, interested but not curious, watched them drive away in the two cars, Baffin riding with Jonathan. She wrote on a slip of paper that the doctor was having supper at the Inn. She thought: Won't that ever please her Highness! And she didn't mean Frances.

58

Chapter Four

It was par for any course that the canary-colored convertible would arrive at the Inn before Jonathan's car. When he drove into the parking space, Frances was leaning over the barrier fence and looking down at the water. He parked, adjusted the windows for Baffin's comfort, and walked over to her.

"Hello," he said.

"Fancy meeting you here," said Frances. "Where have you been all this time?"

"Traffic. Perhaps I had an emergency call."

"Any excuse is better than none. Why don't you buy a new car?"

"Can't afford it."

"I'll give you one for Christmas . . . There's a moon —"

"So I see."

"I wouldn't have dreamed you'd notice. You can't diagnose a moon . . . Let's go in. I'm famished."

In the lobby, where lobsters, mercifully unaware of their destinies, swam in a large lighted tank, the hostess came toward them, smiling. She looked once at Jonathan and spoke his name; she looked twice at Frances ... she'd seen her a time or two, and Frances asked, "Hi, Jenny, how are you?"

Lord, thought Jonathan, she's quite a character. I was beating my brains to remember the girl's name. Yet she came to me twice last season; sunburn, I think. And Jenny wasn't here when Frances stayed at the Inn last spring; she's summer staff.

They had a good table, next to a window; the dinner crowd was beginning to thin out.

"Drink?" he asked.

"No, thanks, one's my limit before dinner. And don't look so astonished."

"Why not? I am, a little."

"I may run with hounds," said Frances, "but I'm a hare at heart."

They ordered and sat watching the glimmer of spun silver on the dark water and the moored boats. And when the order came Frances said, "Now we can talk. I believe in being incautious, candid, and confidential while eating."

"Why?"

"That's one thing I like about you ... you never waste words. Well, for one reason, if the conversation languishes, you can always chew

60

and if you feel you must say something shame-making, as our British friends put it, you can reasonably mumble."

"What is it you want to hear, or, want me to know?"

"I just wanted to say — this is really good chowder — that I know a good deal about you, and at the same time, not much."

"That's a statement you could make about almost everyone."

"Certainly. I know about your family, your background, your medical training; I know about your Navy service and your work in New York; I know about your wife's accident . . ."

He said, "And you're still not being psychic. You got all that from Sophie."

"Of course. Over a long period actually, starting two summers ago. You don't think I cultivated her because she's my type?"

"Frankly," he said, very irritated, "I hadn't given it a thought."

"That time *you* mumbled," she remarked cheerfully. "I'm just saying I wish you'd fill me in a little —"

"There's nothing to —"

"Oh, but there is. Sophie says you blame yourself for your wife's accident."

He said shortly, "Possibly I did for a time — one always does. You think: If I hadn't gone out just before the phone call . . ."

The waitress came to remove the soup cups, the saltines. When she had gone, Frances said, "You were terribly in love with your wife."

He did not answer. He offered her a cigarette and lit it for her; and she said, "So, skip it. I'm sorry I said it."

"That's all right," he said. But it wasn't all right. He resented her question.

Now she asked, "There's been no one else?"

"In what way?"

"That way," she said with a little gesture. "The way that counts."

"No." He added on a rising note of anger, "Not that it's any of your business, Frances."

"I think it is," she said. "Now, it's my turn to mumble — although that wretched girl hasn't brought the lobster yet . . . if there's anything worth mumbling over it's hot boiled lobster. . . . You see, I'm in love with you," she went on thoughtfully, "and a girl likes to know where she stands."

He said roughly, "Look, Frances, I'm not interested in trick or treat —"

"Nor am I. . . . Here comes our relief," she said. "The cavalry to the rescue."

The lobster arrived, the French fries, the green beans and the salad and Frances asked, smiling at the waitress, "May we have coffee now?"

Jonathan said after a moment, "Frances, this is something you've dreamed up because you're bored."

"On the contrary, Doctor, I'm bored *because* I've dreamed it up and can't get anywhere."

Suddenly she seemed about six years old, a crazy, mixed-up, delightfully exasperating little girl. You'd like to shake her until her teeth rattled, or spank her, or . . .

He laughed aloud. "You'll get over it," he predicted.

"Oh, sure," she agreed, working industriously on the lobster. "Antibiotics are marvelous. All the miracle drugs, including one called Time, I believe. As a matter of fact, I know where I stand; exactly in the middle of nowhere and nothing. Perhaps I'd better say, I'd like you to know where you stand. . . ."

"Right here — a hard-working, bad-tempered, sometimes dissatisfied GP with an overload of patients, very little time for himself or anyone else who isn't ill, and a wonderful housekeeper who's a bad cook."

"Also a domineering sister," said Frances. "Not that I don't admire Sophie, at a distance — or would if she'd been painted and hung on a wall in the proper light. She'd give her eye teeth if you married me," she said carelessly.

"She can't spare 'em," said Jonathan.

"Now," said Frances, "you don't know anything about me, except that I'm rich – and incidentally in my own right. I didn't want a shining silver dollar of Charlie's money."

"Charlie?"

"My former husband, Charles Peabody Hamilton the Third."

"I'd forgotten," said Jonathan. "His name, I mean."

"I sometimes do," she said. "You also know that I'm willful and spoiled; that my father lives in a nice, hard, expensive shell and my mother's an alcoholic."

"Frances –"

"Oh, she is," said Frances idly. "She had a go at being treated once and a little fling with AA, but nothing rubbed off. You know her very slightly – keep it that way. She likes young men."

He was silent and presently she said, "Go ahead and tell me I'm sorry for myself. You'd be so right. Perhaps I thought I was in love with Charlie. I know I wanted to get away from the Lawson house, from the several Lawson houses. . . . There was nothing very wrong with Charlie – he was just like most of the men I knew, only more so – a little more money, a little more status, a little less brain. But he was – and I daresay is – a pretty good guy. Maybe if there'd been Charles Peabody Hamilton the Fourth or Frances, Jr., I would have stuck it out. Or longer, anyway. As a matter of fact, there was — never mind which — dead on arrival," she went on colorlessly, "and also as a matter of fact — this is something I wanted to tell you — there'll never be another one. Or so the most expensive members of your profession — in their field — have told me. That's something you ought to know just in case your foot slips and you find yourself falling."

He said gently, "I'm sorry, Frances."

"So am I. Anyway where were we? . . . So I got a divorce. Charlie was upset for a few weeks; his pride was injured. But he recovered nicely and remarried. They're living abroad. He doesn't have to earn his living," said Frances. "Isn't that lovely for him? And I go chasing around looking and looking . . . and, of course, trying to escape, which no one ever does."

As they drank their coffee, she said, "That's all. Don't say I didn't warn you."

A tall man with an unlikely dark beard and startlingly blue eyes came to their table, crying, "Fran, darling!"

Frances said, "Must you barge in, Kim?"

"Thanks," said Mr. Sylvester. "I'd just love to sit down and have a drink with you."

Frances performed the introductions and

65

Kim Sylvester smiled. His teeth were as white as his eyes were blue.

"Aren't you the painter?" asked Jonathan, rescued by interruption.

"Well goody goody gumdrops," Kim caroled. "Fame in my own lousy time. Thank you ever so much."

"Don't be an idiot," Frances advised him crossly. "There's no point in affectation. Doctor Condit is, I think, fully aware that you do not dance ballet on the dunes."

Jonathan was. He had observed the lean, rather brutal jaw line, only partially softened and concealed by the absurd beard, also the good forehead, and the sharp intelligence in the blue eyes.

"I think I saw your paintings last year in the open-air show, Mr. Sylvester," he said.

"Oh, quite. And I met your sister. She wanted to buy one of the lesser masterpieces, but I charge too much, or so she insisted. As for Fran's remark about the ballet dancing — when in Rome, assume an appearance. It can produce amusing reactions. Besides, I hate being conspicuous."

He took Frances' hand and looked at it. "Darling, what an ugly little paw," he commented.

Jonathan found himself looking closely for

the first time at Frances Lawson's hands. They did not suit the rest of her. He'd thought of them, without looking, as graceful and long-fingered. They were not. They were small, and square with short, spatulate fingers.

He said, fascinated, "They don't seem part of her, do they? But you're wrong. They're not ugly, Mr. Sylvester —"

"Call me Kim. It's cosier."

"— on the contrary, they are practical working hands — active and healing. . . . Surgeons have such hands, only bigger," Jonathan went on.

"Most creative people do, too," Kim said, finishing his drink. "This long-fingered artistic hand stuff is for the birds."

The hostess, Jenny, came across the room to report, "There's a call for you, Doctor Condit."

"Lovely timing," said Kim, "so Frances is stuck with the check. I'm never," he added, "since I don't carry money, and I haven't a credit card except for gas."

Jonathan spoke to Frances. He said, "Get the check, will you? I'll be right back."

While he was gone, Kim inquired, "Why aren't you paying the check?"

"He asked me to dinner," she said mendaciously. "Incidentally, I'm not happy to see you."

"You may be someday and I'm predatory. . . .

So, this is the dream prince?"

"Certainly."

"Terrible miscasting," Kim remarked. "Now you get to drive me home, I presume."

"How did you get here?"

"I walked," he answered. "That's what keeps my credit card unsullied."

Jonathan came back. His face was without expression, but Frances asked, "Bad, isn't it?"

"I'm afraid so. I'm sorry, Frances." He paid the check, left the tip and said briefly, "Nice meeting you," to Kim, and to Frances, "Some other time, perhaps."

"Almost certainly," she answered.

He smiled at them with his mouth, but not his eyes, and went out with his long, quiet stride.

"Quite a fella at that," said Kim Sylvester. "How about buying me another drink? Or I'll even buy you one."

"I thought you said you didn't carry money."

"Mother always made sure I had mad money and a clean hankie."

"You're impossible," said Frances and rose.

Kim followed her out to the car. "Gorgeous car," he mused. "Reasonably attractive girl, rich as hell. If you have to support a husband — and I wouldn't settle for less, for long; it's too risky — why must you pick on a noble practitioner of what I'm certain is an inexact science rather than a brilliant, talented and unappreciated painter?"

Frances got into the car. She said, "Get in, idiot, and I'll take you back to your attic."

"Do you wish to come up and hear my supersonic records?"

"No," said Frances. And then added, "By now, since the last several obvious attempts, you must realize that when I listen to records, it is as part of a large audience; also, when I look at paintings, etchings, or watch Karate."

"I do realize it. The last time, for instance, I thought you'd been taking lessons."

It wasn't far to where he had living quarters, across the highway and up a country road where he inhabited, not an attic, but the top floor of an ancient, sagging house.

"Sure you won't come in, darling?"

"Quite sure. And don't call me darling!"

He got out and stood beside the car, moderately tall and immoderately arrogant.

"Good night," he said formally. "Sleep well and if you don't, call a doctor."

Driving home, dismissing Kim Sylvester as irritating and inconsequential as a malicious gnat, she thought of Jonathan. Where was he?'

He was with people whom she knew only

because now and again she went into the hardware store.

It was very late when Jonathan reached home. He had found time to call the house and leave a message for Sophie with Mrs. Parker, who said she'd stay on until Miss Condit came in.

In the Karlin house, after their return from the hospital, Sam Karlin asked dully, "But why, Doc? Why?"

Jonathan shook his head. "Who knows?" he said wearily. "She doesn't know herself."

"We should have listened to you," said Mrs. Karlin, her face broken with shock and grief.

Jonathan might have felt a little vindicated; he did not.

Young Mary Karlin was in the hospital very badly burned. She had been baby-sitting quietly. . . . But there were matches, big kitchen matches in that house.

The neighbors saw the flames creeping up the curtains and one went rushing in while another telephoned the fire department. The one who went in found Mary standing in the middle of the floor . . . "No, not standing," he corrected himself, "but – like dancing. And she was laughing. . . ."

He'd snatched the small child from the playpen, and taken him outside, thrusting him, screaming, into the arms of one of the people who had gathered there. Then he and another man had gone back for Mary.

"It wasn't more than a minute," he'd said, "but she was . . . my God, she was all on fire!"

They'd managed to get her out, to roll her in a rug. . . .

Sophie had waited up and Jonathan told her in short, unadorned sentences what had happened.

"How dreadful!" said Sophie, and brought him a highball. "Here," she said, "drink this. You look like death. . . . Will she recover?"

"From the burns? Yes, I think so, if there are no complications. From what caused her to strike the matches − I − don't − know."

If she recovered, then it was a case for Doctor Marod. What chances of success there would be Jonathan could not tell. . . . If none, then an institution.

He did not think of Frances again until he was almost asleep, and then with the admixture of exasperation, embarrassment, and attraction with which he usually thought of her − when he thought of her at all. Yet now there was a new ingredient, a measure of compassion.

Spoiled and willful she had called herself, and he could agree with her . . . but it was not as easy now to pigeonhole her as just that. He thought drowsily of her parents, and of her husband, whom he had never known and of her inability to bear a living child. He could not dismiss this factor lightly, for she did not.

He wondered if there had been other men. Before tonight he wouldn't have wondered, he would have said, "Yes, of course." But now he wondered – doubted – even debated.

There'd been some talk about her and Kim Sylvester. Jonathan thought: I bet that isn't his name. He could discount the talk now unless – as often happened – there had been something between them, followed by a quarrel. No, he didn't think so. He didn't like the man, but he could see more clearly than most through the stone wall of affectation.

He yawned, and frowned and Baffin padded over to the bed. Jonathan put his hand on the Labrador's head and said, "Go back to sleep. I'm all right."

Drifting off, his final thought was not of Frances Lawson but of Sam Karlin, his wife, and of their daughter Mary in the hospital.

Chapter Five

Leaving the hospital a day or so later Jonathan ran into – almost literally, for he was greatly preoccupied – the pleasant woman from a neighbor town who headed the volunteers.

"I'm sorry," he said. "I wasn't looking where I was going."

Mrs. James smiled. She said, "I can understand that. How is Mary?"

He said heavily, "She'll be all right, but it will be a long haul."

"Tragic," said Mrs. James, "for her, and her parents." Then she said, "I'm grateful to you, Doctor Condit, for inducing Miss Lawson to work with us."

He looked, as he felt, astonished – and amused; he couldn't imagine anyone inducing Frances to do anything she didn't want to do.

"It was her own idea really," he said.

"That," responded Mrs. James, "was not the impression she gave me. When I interviewed her, I gathered that you had practically forced her with a chair and a whip to volunteer."

He laughed and said, "Well, from your earlier remark, I take it she's working out all right."

"She's marvelous," said Mrs. James. "She has just what we need in a volunteer — intelligence, imagination, the ability to follow directions, and she doesn't panic. A time or two, she might have. Miss Lucas agrees with me that Miss Lawson would have made an exceptionally fine nurse. She's particularly good with children, incidentally."

"That's fine," said Jonathan.

He went out into the dazzling sunlight and got into the car greeted by Baffin and drove on home in time for lunch. To his surprise Sophie, erupting from the yard, said, "Olive Evans is waiting to see you."

For a moment he thought: Who? Then remembered. "I told her I'd make an appointment . . ." Sophie went on.

He wasn't listening. He went on into the office with his almost noiseless stride. Olive rose, flushing a little when he spoke to her.

He asked, "Is it your aunt? Has anything happened?"

"Oh, no, she's all right," said Olive. "I tried to explain to Miss Condit that I just wanted some advice — not as a patient. . . ."

"Sit down, Olive," he said. "What can I do for you?"

"It's about the Karlins," she began. Her clear, grave eyes regarded him steadily. "I don't really know them," she said. "I've only been working in the store since I came to be with Aunt Susan. But I'm so sorry for them, Doctor Condit. I'd like to help. Aunt Susan has decided to work evenings. She filled in at first as a favor; now she likes it, I think. She gets to work later and stays later. I just thought — if I could be of help at the Karlin house — but I don't know how to go about it. Mrs. Karlin is at the hospital so much and Mr. Karlin goes evenings. . . . There are things I could do," she said firmly. "Cook supper, for instance; put things shipshape."

Shipshape. That sounded like Pete.

"That's extraordinarily kind of you."

"I've only met Mrs. Karlin a couple of times," Olive told him, "and I know the neighbors do everything they can, but I would like to help."

"How'd you get here?" he asked.

"It's my lunch hour. I got a lift."

"Then stay and have lunch with us," said Jonathan. "After lunch I'll take you back to the store and we can map our campaign on the way."

Sophie didn't as much as lift an eyebrow when he went into the living room, saying cheerfully, "We have a guest. Will you ask Mrs. Parker to set anther place?"

She said, "That's nice," and smiled at Olive. Behind her smile wariness and curiosity. She couldn't remember when Jonathan had done anything like this before. If he wanted someone to lunch or dinner, he usually spoke to her first and she made the arrangements.

As she went into the kitchen, she said to herself: "Oh, *no* . . .!" A nice girl, she assumed, and presentable enough, but surely he couldn't be interested. Not suitable at all, thought Sophie, not at all.

They had lunch and Sophie was pleased to be gracious, drawing from Olive all possible details of her home, her family, her present occupation. She couldn't have been nicer, thought Jonathan, afflicted with a desire to strangle his sister and a contrary desire to laugh.

When Jonathan drove up to the shop and, by some miracle, found a parking space, he went in with Olive. Sam Karlin was alone behind the counter, and Jonathan asked, "Sam, couldn't Mrs. Karlin do with a little assistance?"

Olive stood waiting.

Karlin said, "Folks come in and out. . . ."

He had aged visibly; he spoke as an old man speaks, moved his hands slowly, and had difficulty in focusing his eyes.

"I know," said Jonathan, "but Olive wants to do a little more. You see, her aunt is working evenings . . . and she thought she could make herself useful to you. I bet she's a good cook," he added.

But Karlin began, worried, "We – I mean –"

Olive knew what he meant. She said quickly, "I wasn't asking for a job, Mr. Karlin. You've already given me one. I just thought I could tidy things up and fix supper for you or leave something ready for you to heat up when you came back from the hospital. I'd like to so much."

And it was so arranged, Karlin's face working as he tried to thank her.

As Jonathan left them and went back to his car, he thought: More good people than bad in this idiot world; that's a fine girl.

He was exceptionally busy as summer went along, with its spells of heat, its occasional crushing humidity, then fog and a needed rain, unusual thunderstorms, a spell or two of cold. The office was always crowded. There were house calls. People kept coming down with the so-called summer viruses. There were accidents. And every day he went to the hospital, for he usually had patients there — and Mary, of course.

Mary appeared to have no memory of the fire, except to say, when first she was able to talk, "I burned myself." She said it as a child would say, "I hurt."

"She won't talk to me about it," Mrs. Karlin told Jonathan wretchedly.

"No. How and why it happened is something she has to remember later, if she's to live with herself. Later, when she has physically recovered, I'm certain Doctor Marod can help her to remember. It will be painful for her, but he thinks it's necessary."

On the evenings that Sam Karlin went to the hospital, Olive saw to it that he ate supper. On the days when he went early, he and Mrs. Karlin had a sandwich in the coffee shop and came home after visiting hours to find that Olive had left something for them, and the coffee ready to perk.

"I don't know what we would have done without her," Sam told Jonathan, "and her a stranger."

"Well, look whose niece she is. And she likes helping," Jonathan said.

"She's good in the store, too," Sam said. "I'll sure miss her there when school opens. She says she'll go on doing for us until we don't need her any more — at home that is."

Both Karlin and his wife, sitting through long quiet hours with their daughter, found that she had little to say to them, or for that matter, they to her. She looked at them with recognition, said hello and good-by. Sometimes she talked of things that had happened in her childhood, starting animatedly; then her voice would trail off into silence.

One evening, as the Karlins were leaving the hospital, Jonathan said, "Sam, there's not much use of you and your wife half killing yourself to be here every day."

"I suppose not, but it makes us feel better."

There was, Jonathan knew, a burden of guilt here; it was not one he could lighten. He had tried. "If you're blaming yourself . . ." he'd begun and Sam had snapped at him, "What's there for us to blame ourselves about?"

Twice Jonathan and Sophie had been to dinner at Driftwood. Once he even stayed until eleven without being called out; both times were on his evening off. The first time Mr. Lawson was there; and both times Kim Sylvester.

Kim was highly amused by Frances' hospital work. "Little Miss Nightingale," he called her.

Jonathan observed Maida Lawson with considerable interest. If she were an alcoholic — and he didn't doubt it — she restricted her public intake to something approaching moderation. Before — and after — dinner she probably indulged herself. She was a pretty woman. Frances looked rather like her. Mrs. Lawson was also vivacious, hard, and he thought, driving and driven. With Kim Sylvester — and with any other guests — she exerted herself to be amusing. There were others the nights Jonathan and Sophie were there.

Sophie had made up her mind that she did not like Kim. "Not that he isn't talented," she told Jonathan as they drove away the second night. "I'd give my eye teeth to have that dune painting of his, but he wanted the earth for it. That idiotic manner of his," Sophie continued, "is just put on. Anyone can see that. But he's after Frances and I don't like it."

"Frances can handle him," said Jonathan.

"Maybe so. . . . It's her money, of course," said Sophie with a snort.

"Come, come," said Jonathan. "Frances is a very attractive young woman and would be if she hadn't a dime."

It was dark so he couldn't see his sister look at him sharply, but he felt it as if she'd stuck a pin in him.

"Well, I'm glad you admit it finally!"

"I've never denied it," Jonathan said blandly.

"Also," said Sophie, "Maida Lawson is

making a fool of herself over Kim."

"Is she?"

"Jonathan, I could shake you!"

"Not when I'm driving —"

"Of course she is — all this looking up from under lashes business and her hand on his arm with or without excuse — you must have noticed — it's disgusting."

"It's her business," he said shortly. He had noticed, of course. It had made him feel faintly sick, and very much embarrassed; for Maida, for Frances and, on the first occasion, for Mr. Lawson.

Well, it would be Labor Day soon and after that, the great exodus, the emptying of roads, highways, beaches, summer cottages. Then the influx of the late vacationers, with no children or grown children, who would come in the velvet autumn, with the trees exploding into color, with the warm days and the cold nights. After they'd gone Seascape would hibernate.

He was not prepared for Frances' announcement when one day he saw her in the hospital that she was staying on.

"For how long?" he asked, astonished.

"Oh, the autumn, possibly the winter. . . . I don't know. There's nowhere I want to go," said Frances, "so I may as well stay on here."

"In that elegant barn?"

"No, the guesthouse. You've never seen it, have you? . . . The works, including heat and a little kitchen. I'll cook dinner for you sometime."

Then she was gone, walking swiftly down the corridor.

Nor was he prepared for Susan Jarvis' telephone call, just after Labor Day. She said she'd like to see him. Could she stop by on her way to work?

It was so arranged and when she sat facing him at the desk, he saw that she looked anxious. She did not, however, look ill. He asked, "What's wrong, Susan?"

"Nothing, with me. I'm just fine. Work," she said as if to herself, "that's the answer. I'll miss it, but I'll find something else."

The small restaurant was closing around October first.

He waited and presently she said with some difficulty, "It's Olive. . . ."

"Olive? Doesn't she like her job? . . . Oh, I know she hasn't been at the school long but —"

"She likes it; and everyone likes her. But there's — well — talk."

"Talk?"

"About her and Sam Karlin."

"For heaven's sake!" said Jonathan, erupting into anger. "What kind of talk?"

"About – this summer – and now her still going there when Emily Karlin's at the hospital – and him home alone and all."

"Susan!" He thought he'd choke. He said, "You can't believe it."

"Oh, I don't," she said quietly, "but Olive's got a mind of her own and when I spoke to her, she just gave me an odd sort of look. I know she started helping out because she's a kind girl and a good one, but the neighbors –"

"The hell with the neighbors," said Jonathan. Yet he was conscious of uneasiness. "All the girl's been doing is to act like one."

"Which she isn't," Susan reminded him. "You don't have to take up for her. I know her. All I'm asking is, would you speak to her about it? You can."

Jonathan said, "Mary will be going home soon. After a while she'll go back for some skin grafts, but while she's home Olive won't be needed –"

"She thinks she will," said Olive's aunt. "She thinks she can still help. She's got some kind of a bee in her bonnet about the whole family."

Jonathan said, "All right, I'll speak to her. But exactly how –"

Susan knew what he meant. She said, "Well, she won't come here, that's for sure, but if you could stop by one evening before the restaurant closes?"

So he did, not liking the idea at all.

Olive was at home, back from the Karlins', if indeed she'd been there. She had bought a little third-hand car to get herself to school and back. The car was out in the yard as Jonathan drove up.

He knocked and she opened the door. She said, smiling, "Hello, Doctor. Aunt Susan's out, I'm sorry to say."

"I suppose so. But I came to see you."

Olive regarded him a moment, warily, he thought. Then she said, "Do come in, Doctor."

"Try Jonathan for size," he said casually. "I'm not your doctor, you know. Or not yet; and hope I won't be; you appear to be in top-flight condition. Also, if you mean to accord me respect, I was born later than you think."

He followed her as she headed toward the stiff little parlor, veered, and led the way into the kitchen. Her supper dishes were rinsed and stacked in the sink. A coffeepot sat squarely over a low flame on the stove, and Jonathan looked at Pete's easy chair and at a rocker from which, evidently, Olive had just risen as it was still in motion. . . . Both seemed to be yawning at him.

"How many times," he commented, "boy and man — to coin a phrase — have I sat in this kitchen." He was tired, he thought, and therefore fanciful. This was a diagnosis he had offered many patients. "You're bushed; you need a rest; you're imagining things." Yet he could see, back of his eyes, Pete Jarvis in the shabby old armchair, looking at him through the clear distance-seeing eyes, the glasses sliding down his nose.

Abruptly the walls shrank, crowded in, and he said, "Will you come out with me, Olive? I've a house call to make. We can have a little ride and talk in the car."

"Coffee first?" she asked.

"No thanks."

She turned off the burner under the pot and picked up a heavy sweater from the back of the rocking chair. It was a star-dominated night, sweet and cold.

They went to the car and Baffin spoke amiably to Olive. He had nothing against her except that three's a crowd. With resignation, he left the front seat and thumped over into the back.

As Jonathan drove off, he said apologetically, "I won't be long and it's no emergency. Do you know the Mantons?"

"I've a couple of the girls in my classes," she said.

"It's Wilma — aches, a little temperature. . . ."

85

He was silent then, listening to the sound of the surf. A plane went over, lights flashing, and Olive said, "I suppose Aunt Susan asked you to talk to me?"

"That's right."

She said, "I'm sorry she's upset."

"Aren't you?"

"Why no," she answered. "Why should I be? I haven't done – I'm not doing – anything wrong."

"This is a small place," he said, "and people gossip."

"They do anyplace," she said scornfully. "All I've done is give the Karlins a hand."

"I realize that, Olive, and so does your aunt. But the School Board may not."

She said defensively, "Mrs. Karlin's such an unhappy little woman –"

Jonathan broke in. "Has she a first name? I never remember it, yet she's been to me as a patient and with Mary."

"It's Emily," said Olive. "I don't call her that. She ... I suppose you know she hasn't many friends, not close, that is?"

"No. I didn't."

"Neighbors, of course," said Olive. "But her whole life's bound up in Mary."

"I know."

"If she had other children," Olive

began, "if she and Sam —"

Sam, he thought. But not *Emily*.

"It would be different. Oh, I don't mean that it wouldn't be just as dreadful — only different," Olive concluded.

He said, "I don't know the Karlins well. I've hardly known them at all except professionally — until now."

She said, "He's a good man, Doctor —"

"What did I tell you?"

"Jonathan, then." She said the name doubtfully, as one tries some new exotic dish, finding it strange to the palate, "And lonely."

After a moment he said, "I'm not trying to interfere. I'm warning you, that's all. It isn't a good combination, you know, an overdevoted mother, a lonely man, and an attractive young woman."

"That's ridiculous," she said shortly.

He said, "Part of their situation is guilt, Olive."

"Guilt?"

He said uncomfortably, since ethics are ethics, "Mary should have been under observation long ago; the Karlins were against it. On that they agreed."

She said, "I know. Sam told me and he does blame himself for the — the accident."

Jonathan's heart constricted. He said, "We all

blame ourselves for something, I suppose."

They reached the Manton house, which was on a small street just outside the village and he said, "You and Baffin wait here, like good children."

As he went into the house he thought: She is a good child; but stubborn, like many good children.

When he came out, Baffin was in the front seat with his head in Olive's lap.

"Well, well," said Jonathan, "the minute my back's turned!"

Baffin laughed and Jonathan said, "You old sweet-talking monster. Over!"

Obediently Baffin went over and Jonathan remarked, getting into the car, "He's a little crowding when I have someone in the front seat with me."

"How's Wilma?"

"She thinks she's dying," he said, "but it's mainly of resentment. She had a date tonight."

They were silent, leaving the quiet street, turning into the main street of town, which was also quiet. Even the highway which they crossed was negotiable.

Presently he said, "I hope you'll think over what I said. I appreciate your situation, I applaud your generosity, but I don't want to see you hurt; and even more, I don't want your aunt hurt. She's not young, my dear; she's adjusting to losing about three-quarters of herself, and making a good job of it."

Olive said shortly, "All right, I won't go over anymore. I don't really suppose they'll need me when Mary gets home. I just thought maybe I could help her."

"I didn't advise you to stop seeing them altogether," he said. "As for Mary, I'd wait until someone asks you; specifically, her mother. It may be that she will need some assistance. I've arranged for the district nurse to come in every day, but there might be errands or something. . . . Play it by ear, will you? But listen carefully."

"All right. But it's pretty silly." Then she said, "I've been through this before, you know."

He was so astonished that he nearly missed a turn. "You have?" he asked.

"At home — a couple of houses away," she explained. "A man I'd known all my life. His wife died. There were children. . . . I used to go over."

Well, my God, a pattern! Jonathan thought. Aloud, he said, "And people talked?"

"My parents did a little more than that."

"I see."

Once bitten, twice shy? Like most adages it didn't hold one hundred per cent.

"Your aunt knew this?"

"Oh, yes," she said acidly, "everyone knew. My — my father likes to talk, too. He said I was trying to make Carl marry me."

"And were you?" asked Jonathan evenly.

"No." She waited a moment. Then, "I wasn't in love with him, Doctor — Jonathan. The kids were at the crazy half-grown stage — and before his sister came on from California to look after them they were — well, you know teen-agers."

"Some," he admitted. "How old was — his name is Carl?"

She said, "A lot older than I am; he married late, I guess. . . . She was quite young — his wife, I mean."

Sam Karlin was a lot older, too.

Olive said defensively, "He and the children needed me until things got straightened out."

The need to be needed, he thought. It expresses itself all the time, sometimes in beauty, sometimes not. . . . Who knows another's motive?

He took her home. A light was on where none had been, which meant that Susan was home; one of her fellow workers picked her up and drove her to and from work.

"Won't you come in?" Olive was out of the car, leaning in at the window and he said, "Not tonight, thanks."

She looked very young in the uncertain light. Vulnerable and appealing. Oh, hell . . . the poor kid!

He moved over, leaned out, and kissed her lightly. He said, "Good night. Think over what I said."

She did not answer; she was running up the path, the bulky sweater slung across her slim shoulders.

Baffin barked — once.

"And no wonder," said Jonathan aloud, proceeding home. "Now what did I do that for? Of all the damned fool . . ."

Yet he knew. . . . He was suspectible to youth and vulnerability; not that Olive reminded him of Edna in any other way.

Chapter Six

A few days later he stopped by one morning to see Susan. Mary Karlin had come home in the town ambulance. He told Susan so and added, "I had a talk with Olive. She suspected that you'd asked me to."

"I know. She said so, and as much as told me to mind my own business, but she's not going to that house any more. Except yesterday, when Mary came home, she went over with some of my peach-plum jelly and a custard."

He said after a moment, "Don't worry about her. She has a good head on her shoulders. She just likes to be helpful."

Susan said wearily, "Pete used to call people like Olive do-gooders."

"Well, hasn't she done good?"

"Not always," said Susan. "I don't suppose she told you about the trouble with her father over the man who lived near them? And still does," she added. "He married again, last spring."

Jonathan raised an eyebrow. "As a matter of fact she did tell me."

"It beats everything," Susan said. "She had a half a dozen boys chasing after her at home. There's one or two started to here."

"She's attractive," he said and reflected that he had not thought her so until she smiled. These quiet girls, the ones you think plain, he informed himself — well, the honey's in an unornamental container, but somehow the bees discover it.

"It will work out. . . . You're looking tired, Susan."

"I'm all right. And the work isn't too hard." She smiled wryly. "They spare me, I think. Or try to. But even with Olive here, it's lonesome."

He nodded. He said, "For me, too, even with friends like you to talk to."

"Pete thought the world of you," she said.

He wondered, driving off, what particular bee Olive had attracted. He hoped he was good enough for her.

Which made him think of do-gooders.

He found himself in a mute mental argument with Pete. Not all do-gooders, he told his friend, come under your rather disdainful category; not all are motivated by whatever you thought motivated them — vanity, the desire to play God — not all are merely interfering. . . .

Still the pattern bothered him; the older man, the desire to soothe, cosset, spoil.

That night in the office, just as he had put the last stitch in a small brown hand while its owner was yelling his red head off to the distress of his anxious mother, the telephone rang. He reached for it and a voice said, "Jon? It's Frances. Please get here as soon as you can."

"What —"

"Mother," she said. "Don't talk. Hurry."

So he said to two people, both chronics, who were waiting for him, "It's an emergency. I don't know when I'll be back." And he said to the small boy's mother, "He'll be all right. Bring him to see me tomorrow." Then he grabbed his bag and tore out, shouting at Sophie over his shoulder, "Emergency."

The Lawson house blazed with lights, so did the guesthouse, and Frances came flying out to meet him.

"What happened?"

"Whisky and sleeping pills."

What he could do, he did, and Mrs. Lawson's maid, Cecile, and Frances helped him. Frances was very white and her lips were a straight hard line, the rouge chewed off unevenly.

Jonathan had called the ambulance and Frances rode with her mother. Jonathan following.

In the emergency room Frances said, "I'll have to tell my father."

"I'm afraid so," Jonathan said, as if she'd asked a question.

He managed to get a private room and discreet nurses. He put Frances out in the reception room to wait; and one of the residents worked with him. It was a narrow thing, and very unpleasant.

When he came out, Frances was walking about, furiously smoking, and he said. "O.K., she'll do."

"I'll spend the night. I can stay out here if there's no place to put me."

"There isn't and you may as well go home. We were lucky to get that room." He grinned crookedly. "There's always one on tap for a VIP."

"I know. Sometimes it enrages me, but not tonight. I'd hate to have her with anyone . . . she'll talk, you know."

They were on the way out now and he said, "I didn't know, but it's not unusual."

"This isn't the first time," said Frances.

In his car she said savagely, "She's such a little fool. She has everything."

"That's what you think. Obviously, she hasn't."

"I suppose not. Recently it was Kim Sylvester

she wanted. Then she found that, after his fashion, he wanted me."

"Suppose you don't tell me—"

"Why not? You're her doctor."

"Pro tem, Frances. . . ."

She said, "My father will raise the roof. He swore that if this happened again, or even if she just went on as she's been doing, he'd send her to an institution."

He said, "I'll talk with him. Look, I forgot in all the excitement, what's she doing here? I thought she'd gone back to town."

"She went back and then returned here. No warning. She drove in as if she were in a drag race late this afternoon. Her maid was with her."

"Yes, I saw her."

"She left Cecile in the house — it's no trouble to open up — the furnace is left on. She wouldn't stay in the guesthouse with me. She went out — I suppose to see Kim. Then she came back early. I heard her crash in; the gravel must be scattered for half a mile. She slammed the door, but not before I heard her stumble. She must have taken the stuff at once —"

"And plenty of it," said Jonathan.

"It hit her fast," said Frances, "empty stomach probably, except for the whisky."

When they drove into the Driftwood grounds, he said, "I'll come in a moment. I cleared out my office patients. You look as if you could do with a moderate drink."

"No, thanks."

"And," he added, "a moderate sleeping pill."

"I'll sleep all right," she said. "I'll be at the hospital tomorrow – after all I'm working there."

"Shall I call your father from here?"

"No. That's nice of you, Jon, but I'd better, I guess." She sat down, then jumped up at once. "I must speak to Cecile; she'll be frantic – wait for me."

She went out through the breezeway and he looked around the guest cottage: big living room, fireplace. Probably bedroom with bath. Screened pool, the works. Wandering about, he discovered the little kitchen with its dining corner.

Frances came in. She said, "I gave Cecile the sleeping pill. She was helpful, didn't you think? But she's all to pieces now . . . How about coffee?"

"Sure you can make it?"

"Of course. And I make the best omelette this side of Paris where, incidentally, I learned to make omelettes. . . . I saw you talking to a policeman, Jon."

He had hoped she hadn't. He said, "It's routine, you know."

"Well?"

He said, "So, accidental overdose, naturally."

In some cases the police might not accept it; but with Mrs. Lawson of Driftwood . . . yes, indeed.

Frances made good coffee, strong and black. They drank it together in the living room. He asked, setting down his cup, "You'll be all right?"

"Oh, sure."

"I'll be at the hospital tomorrow as usual. Had there been any necessity, I'd have stayed tonight."

"I know."

As he rose, she rose, too, and moved toward him. She said wearily, "It's all so stupid and so unnecessary." She put her head against him and his arms held her for a moment. Then she said, "Thanks. I wasn't trying to take advantage . . ." She smiled, and he noticed for the first time that she'd restored her lipstick. "It's — well, I'm tired."

"That's all right. I'll see you. Call me if you're worried or scared or can't sleep or whatever."

She kissed his cheek. "Thanks, Jon," she said.

He went home, sorrier for her than he'd thought possible. Sophie was, of course, up.

Where had he been? What had happened?

She'd know soon enough, everyone would know. He said, "To the Lawsons ... Mrs. Lawson's ill. I've put her in the hospital."

"What –" She stopped and asked no further. She'd find out someday, she thought.

In the guesthouse Frances replaced the receiver after talking with her father. . . . No, there was no point in his flying up; it would complicate matters. . . . Yes, she'd call him every day. . . . Yes, if he insisted, he could call Jonathan Condit. . . . No, there was no reason to send McKenzie up. When her mother was able to come home, she, Frances, would drive her, and fly back. No, there was no need to send their own doctor. Jonathan was perfectly capable of handling this, so was the hospital.

The wire had crackled and crackled. Now she sat there with the merciful silence about her and sweat at the roots of her hair.

Then she picked up the telephone and dialed a local number. Kim Sylvester's. But she hung up before completing the call. She was an idiot, she told herself. How could she have considered calling Kim Sylvester to tell him what she thought of him? Besides his telephone was on a party line.

She felt cold and shaky. Perhaps Kim

wouldn't even hear about this . . . No, he'd hear all right. But if she didn't confront him with it, he could not . . .

She remembered a conversation after her mother had returned to the city and Kim had come strolling uninvited into the guest cottage.

"Hello."

She'd said hello; she hadn't asked him to come in, but he had. "Mind?"

"I do, very much. I'm tired and don't feel chatty."

"Nice little rabbit hutch," he had remarked, looking around. "How long will you occupy it?"

"I don't know."

He sat down and laughed at her. He said. "How come so orthodox, Fran? You look" – and he had regarded her from the top of her silver-gold hair to the heels of her slippers – "frightened. How flattering. Virginal, too. How do you manage that? . . . Well, would you consider a paying guest?"

"I would not."

"Oh!" he said softly. "Just for meals, dinners, perhaps?"

To his surprise – and her own – she began to laugh.

"I'm funny?"

"Hilarious. But mainly, obvious. Do go, Kim."

He rose. "I've always been made welcome in the senior house, so to speak," he reminded her.

"I can't very well ask my mother to keep you off her guest list," Frances said, and now she was not laughing. "Although, if you're around next summer – and she is – I can always absent myself."

"Your mother," said Kim, "is a charming woman. A little – er – unstable, but charming. And, although she is not the rose –"

"Oh, get out," she'd cried at him and, smiling a little, he had gone.

In the hospital Maida Lawson talked with Jonathan.

Frances had brought her mother nightgowns, a bedjacket, and an assortment of cosmetics. Maida, sitting up in bed, looked drawn and white, but still pretty. And when Jonathan asked – having sent the nurse from the room – "Do you feel up to talking yet?" she said, "I suppose so."

He waited. Then she asked sharply, "Why don't you ask why I did it?"

"Did you?" he inquired.

"Of course. And do you know why?"

"No," said Jonathan. He looked at her thoughtfully. "You'd had quite a lot to drink," he suggested.

"Oh, that." She shrugged her thin shoulders. "It could be a contributing factor."

"How much did Frances tell you about me?"

He said, "Only what she thought necessary."

"She's in love with you," said Maida indifferently. "But she'll recover, too." She looked at him curiously as if he were a new specimen under a scientist's microscope. "Apparently you don't reciprocate?"

He said quietly, "I didn't come here to talk about Frances."

"I know you didn't," said Maida. "Ah, well — hard-to-get men are always the most challenging. . . . Maybe you won't believe me, but I'm actually very fond of Frances — even if I don't show it. I'm not demonstrative."

A little flicker passed across his face. She saw it.

"I'm talking about myself as a mother," she said. "I'm not particularly maternal. Frances and I are good friends. We quarrel," she said, with vast indifference. "But, then, who doesn't?"

He said, "To get back to why you took the sleeping pills — at, I may add, an unusually early hour."

"I was drunk," she said calmly, "and bored, *bored*, BORED. Have you ever been bored, Jonathan?"

"Not often."

"I'm bored," she said, "most of the time; with my husband, with my daughter, and with myself. And when you're bored, you look for remedies. Sometimes they lighten the boredom for a time, sometimes they don't. I suppose my husband knows what happened — if you call it that. . . ."

"Naturally," said Jonathan. "I offered to talk with him but Frances called him herself that night. Yesterday he talked with me. It wasn't a particularly satisfactory conversation. He is, of course, deeply concerned."

"Oh, skip it," she said. "Concerned isn't the word, is it?"

"What is the word?"

"Angry," she told him, "enraged . . . It isn't the first time. Perhaps he told you that?"

"Yes."

"So what?" she inquired. "Back to the city, back to the doctors who understand my interesting case; back to the pleas of the medical profession. 'Dear Mrs. Lawson, I'm sure you could be greatly helped at Home Harbor or Loving Lodge Care or whatever the place is called . . . but, of course, you'll have to cooperate, you'll have to want to be helped.' Well," she said, looking at him with dark-circled brown eyes, "perhaps I don't want to be helped.

If I want to go to hell in a handbasket, that's my business."

"Yes," said Jonathan, "it is; but I think you'll admit, it's also your husband's business and Frances' too, to some extent."

"Oh, Harry!" she said. "He couldn't care less except that my irresponsibility and excesses upset his social life. . . . Frances" — she hesitated — "yes, she cares, I suppose." And added, half under her breath, "But nobody cares enough."

Jonathan was silent.

She said, "Story of my life? It's simple. Poor, proud, and out of the top drawer. Harry is rich, arrogant, and from somewhere near the bottom. It was an excellent match; my parents were delighted, so were his. I dislike him very much," she said idly, "and always have."

"There were things you could do about that," he suggested.

"Such as divorce? . . . Well, no. In the first place, having bought something with my poverty, pride, and cerulean blood, why give it up? I like having money. In the second place, from a time not too long after Frances was born, I couldn't have gotten a divorce unless Harry wanted me to — and he didn't. But *he* could have."

"I see."

"I doubt that. Did he tell you when he talked to you — who called whom by the way?"

"He called me."

"Charge him for it," she said. "He can afford it. . . . Did he tell you I am a frigid woman?"

"We did not discuss you except as my temporary patient."

"Well, he will if you ever talk to him again." She laughed — a hard, clear sound like crystal breaking. Then she asked, "How public is the little episode?"

"I hope not public at all." He rose and looked down at her. He said, "When I made my report I — stretched the truth somewhat."

"It's easy," said Maida Lawson. "All I have to say is I was tired, I felt ill, I took some sleeping pills and went to sleep; I woke, half dazed and not remembering I'd taken them, so I took some more. That worked last time, to all intents and purposes."

He said, "You'll be going home in a day or so."

"I like it here, oddly enough."

"This room is needed," he told her. "All the space we can get is needed — by sick people."

"So, I'm not sick?"

"Oh, you're sick all right," said Jonathan. "You are, I think, very ill. But you don't need this hospital room or bed. I'll tell Frances; she can come for you tomorrow."

"Your bedside manner," said Maida Lawson, "goes Ben Casey's one better."

"Thank you." He rang for the nurse, said, "Goodby, Mrs. Lawson. I'll sign you out tomorrow and see you before you go."

As the nurse came in and Jonathan went out, he heard his patient murmur, "Poor Frances."

Frances was waiting in the reception room. She said, "I took five minutes off. How is she?"

"She'll live," said Jonathan shortly.

"Oh?" said Frances. "She has that effect on you?"

"I'm afraid so. You can take her home tomorrow. I'd advise you to keep her there a day, perhaps two, before she returns to the city. And stay with her. Move back into the big house, Frances."

"All right. May I see her? She wouldn't see me yesterday."

"You may, of course. There's a 'no visitors' edict, but it doesn't apply to you."

"After I get her home – I'll drive her – I'm coming back, Jon. Shall I see you?"

"Certainly you'll see me." He paused and she said, "You're wondering why I don't do my filial duty and stay at home with her, aren't you?"

106

"No, actually, I'm not."

"I've tried," said Frances, "and tried. It doesn't do a bit of good. I can't help her, Jon."

He was leaving the hospital when Kim Sylvester came from the parking space and said, "Well, hello."

Jonathan asked, "Going somewhere?"

"Kind friend, good car, so I asked to be dropped off here and picked up later."

"Calling on someone?"

"Oh, come," said Kim. "Don't be willful."

"If you have come to see Mrs. Lawson," said Jonathan, "you can't. She's not to have visitors while she is here. Incidentally, how did you know she was here?"

"I have my sources," said Kim. "You'd be surprised. . . . Suppose we let her decide whether she'll see me or not?"

Jonathan took Kim's arm in a hard, bruising grip. "I'd be happy to drive you back to Seascape if your friend has gone on somewhere," he said.

Kim Sylvester was tall; Jonathan taller. And Kim said, "Well, you needn't twist my arm. I'll see her after she gets home, I daresay."

"Until she does," said Jonathan, "my orders will be followed."

"How amusing," said Kim. "The strong silent

type." He wrenched away from Jonathan, ran across the driveway and up the hospital steps. Jonathan followed without haste.

The pretty girl at the information desk was saying, "I'm sorry, Mrs. Lawson isn't permitted visitors." She looked a little bemused. Mr. Sylvester's charm was showing. Then she glanced up and said, "Here's Doctor Condit now."

"We've met," said Sylvester. "No dice, Doctor?"

"None," said Jonathan and added, "and that goes for everyone, Miss Clancy, except, of course, members of Mrs. Lawson's family."

He turned and left, Kim trailing in his wake. "How about the lift?" asked Jonathan pleasantly.

"No thanks. I've friends in this town and I know where to reach the man who brought me. . . . Always get your own way?"

Jonathan said, "It's a good hospital, Mr. Sylvester."

"I see. Wouldn't care to tell me what happened to poor Maida? When I last saw her, of course, she was polluted."

Jonathan said, "I don't discuss my patients."

As he got into his car — with Sylvester looking after him, hands in his pockets, the

wind blowing his dark hair, — he said something short and unattractive, so violently that
Baffin's double coat rose in horror.

"I apologize," said Jonathan to his dog. "Let's
go, shall we? We'll stop somewhere and buy you
an ice cream cone."

Chapter Seven

Jonathan saw Maida Lawson at Driftwood in the late afternoon of the day she went home. He had just seen Mary Karlin and was in no mood for whimsy.

Maida was in her vast bedroom which overlooked salt marsh, shining waters, and gardens which still showed color — late-blooming roses, mauve and pink mums, asters, marigolds.

She was lying on a beautiful old chaise with a foam of mohair across her feet. She looked better; and she was animated and casual. Frances was there wearing a tweed skirt and a pullover. Jonathan thought she had lost weight.

Kim Sylvester was there also.

"I'm fine," said Maida to Jonathan. "These twenty-four hour viruses — you think you're going to die, but you don't."

"They can be very uncomfortable," Jonathan agreed.

"You can say that again. Now, don't bother . . . Frances brought me home — tenderly, as it says in the ballad; Kim dropped in to console. You're fired, Doctor. I feel marvelous."

He said, "That's good. I looked in just to be sure." He added that he had talked to her doctor in the city.

She said carelessly, "How exciting for you. Will you have a drink before you go?"

Jonathan said, "No thanks."

"As Frances is so involved in her emotionally fulfilling hospital duties," said Kim, "I've offered to drive Maida back to the city."

Frances said, "That's kind and sacrificial of you, Kim. But as I've already explained, my father expects me."

Her beautiful mouth normally shaped like a kiss was a straight, thin line, harshly red against her pallor.

"So dull," murmured Maida. Then she said, "Wait a minute, Jon — and you two — clear out."

They cleared, Kim wearing his slight practiced smile.

"Well," said Maida, "the twenty-four-hour virus! How about it? I wonder if he believed me."

"I wouldn't know."

"What I told you in the hospital," she remarked, "was purest eyewash. I was still — shall we say 'under the influence?' Anyway, I was talking off the top of my head."

111

She looked as cool as the fresh autumn wind, except that her eyes were strained and anxious.

He said, "I've forgotten what you said, Mrs. Lawson."

"Harry –" she began, "my husband –"

Jonathan broke in. He said, "You already know I talked to him and to Doctor Stairs."

"So, no twenty-four-hour virus for them. . . . Yes, I know of course." She seemed visibly to brace herself. "The next round's on me." She smiled briefly. "Goodby, and thanks. I mean it, in an academic sort of way. I'm not really grateful for the U.S. Cavalry . . . sometimes it's better if you're left to the Indians. Look after Frances," she said. "I think she's quite mad to stay here, but she's her own mistress and hasn't, to my knowledge, ever been anyone else's. There's not much to amuse her in town and she's fed up with Europe. She has friends here – you, for instance – and her so-called work."

"I'm told that she works hard," said Jonathan.

"No doubt. She always plays her roles to the hilt; dutiful, if eccentric, daughter; noble wife; angel of mercy. . . . And Kim's here, of course."

He said, "Good-by, Mrs. Lawson. Have a good trip."

"You don't like Kim, do you?"

He said, "I don't know him."

"If you did, you'd like him even less," said Maida.

She held out her hand. He took it briefly, then went from the room and downstairs.

Kim was standing by the enormous fireplace with a drink in his hand. Frances was idly rearranging a tall vase of asters.

Jonathan said, "Good-by, Frances — take it easy on the road."

"I shall." She went to the door with him. "Shall I phone?" she asked.

"I'd like that."

"All right." She drew herself up, looking taller than she was. She said, "It's not going to be easy, when we get there."

"I know. If I can help . . . my conversations with your father and with Doctor Stairs weren't exactly satisfactory."

"They wouldn't be. Thanks, Jon, for everything. I'll be back as soon as possible. . . . Perhaps you'll really let me cook dinner for you, some night, when you are free?"

He said, "It's a date," and went with Baffin to his car. He thought: How Maida Lawson hates Frances! She's fond of her, she says, and she probably thinks she is, but she really hates her.

It would have been a splendid idea to punch Mr. Sylvester in the nose. But Jonathan was in no position to do so.

He was already in the car when Kim came loping out and called, "Hi, wait."

Jonathan waited, the engine running. And Kim said, "The lift you offered me recently — how about it, now?"

"How do you get to places?" asked Jonathan with valid curiosity.

"Oh, friends, or I walk. I like walking. But I have a date. . . . I decided it when I didn't get asked to dinner."

He got into the car and Baffin, leaping into the back seat spoke to him amiably, to Jonathan's annoyance.

Kim reached back and scratched Baffin behind the ears. "Nice dog," he said. He looked at Jonathan, his bright blue eyes amused. "It astonishes you," he said astutely, "that so good a judge of character as a dog — especially your dog — does not immediately bite me. . . . But as a matter of fact all dogs like me. So do children, cats, old women" — he paused slightly — "and young. I like them, too. Men don't like me," said Kim, "but that doesn't disturb me. . . . I'd like to paint your portrait," he ended abruptly.

Jonathan laughed. He said, "I'm afraid I haven't time."

"I'm sure you haven't. I can, however, see it . . . grave, virile, and with a certain old-fashioned elegance. Portrait of the young physician. . . . Do you wear glasses?"

"No."

"How amazing! I'd paint you with them, however, held negligently in one hand. You have very fine hands."

"Thanks."

"You do dislike me," said Kim happily.

"I don't know —" Jonathan began and then stopped. "I certainly do," he said.

"Because of Frances, or her mother, or perhaps both?"

"Because," said Jonathan, "of Doctor Fell."

"Pity," Kim murmured. "I rather like you. That is to say you are not exactly my cuppa tea, but you're a trustworthy sort of higher animal. If I get a twenty-four-hour virus I'll come to you. . . ."

"Do," said Jonathan.

"I didn't know it could hospitalize the victim," said Kim. "Look, when you turn into town, let me off. My date's the nearest bar."

He did not speak again until Jonathan stopped the car. Then he said, "I really don't think it was my fault that Maida Lawson tried to escape from what little reality she has. As I told you, she had been hitting the bottle. That we had a small argument wasn't a factor, really."

Jonathan said, "I'd rather not discuss Mrs. Lawson."

"Ah, ethics!" said Kim. "How does it feel to be ethical? What I'm trying to say is, I haven't the least sense of guilt. And I'm sorry for Maida in my horrid little way. She doesn't really want me, you know; at least not for keeps. She simply doesn't want me to horse around after Fran — and Fran doesn't either."

He opened the door and got out. He said, "I'll be seeing you."

Impossible man — devious, amoral, egotistical, and yet . . . What the hell's really the matter with him? thought Jonathan. So under the bubbles, the champagne's flat.

When, a few days later, Kim's painting of the dunes arrived for Sophie, she was completely astonished. It was small, and quite enchanting.

The card read: "You liked this. Please accept it from me."

"But why on earth . . ." said Sophie, helpless for once.

"Who brought it?" asked Jonathan.

"The Simons boy after school. Kim Sylvester has their attic apartment."

Jonathan said, "I'll send him a check."

Sophie said vigorously, "You'll do no such thing. We'll buy something of his at the next show."

116

Jonathan looked at the painting: color, perspective, delicacy — a feeling of the sea and sand. He thought: That's what's the matter, or partly anyway. He's a good painter, but second-rate. He knows he's not first-rate and it's destroying him.

He left Sophie to deal with her thank-you-so-much note and reflected that this episode would probably mean the presence of Mr. Sylvester at the Condit dinner table one evening; and serve him right, he thought. But Sophie had said that night, leaving Driftwood, that she disliked Kim Sylvester.

No doubt he knew it, and the gift of the picture was quite a gesture. Sophie was no different from other women, she was susceptible to attention, even to flattery.

Frances telephoned that they had reached town safely and that her father and Doctor Stairs would be conferring. She added she'd be back as soon as she could.

When she returned to the guest house, she called again to ask, "So, how about dinner?"

He was busy; it wasn't, he said, easy to promise, but as far as he knew on his free evening, yes. He'd probably have to go out shortly after, or even during, dinner.

It was finally arranged and Sophie, hearing that Jonathan would be dining out — and where

– said, "That's nice."

"You have little feathers all over your mouth," her brother told her.

"I have? . . . Oh, don't be an idiot, Jonathan," she said crossly.

He said, "Actually, I think she wants to talk to me about her mother."

"You never did tell me what happened."

"Twenty-four-hour virus," he said evenly.

Sophie permitted herself a slight smile. She said, "Have it your way. It's all over town that she went to Kim Sylvester's apartment and they had – words. Everyone in the house heard them."

Jonathan said, "Words, as you express it, have nothing to do with virus."

"Hits you suddenly, doesn't it?" mused Sophie.

Frances cooked dinner in the guesthouse; a little dinner, the sort that does not keep the hostess too long away from her guests; a very dry Martini, a cup of soup – "canned," she said, "so convenient" – and excellent steak with the usual accompaniments.

After they had dined on the gate-legged table in the living room, Frances said, "Now, you can help me clear away and we'll have coffee."

During dinner she had not spoken of Maida;

118

she had asked him about Mary Karlin – now back in the hospital for the skin grafts – and about other patients of his whom she knew.

Baffin had come in at Frances' invitation and was sleeping in front of a blazing beautiful fire.

During coffee she said, "Well, my father is taking my mother on a cruise."

Jonathan raised an eyebrow, and said nothing.

"There was some talk," she went on, "about the sanitarium, which put her in what is known as a tizzy. Doctor Stairs, always one to find the polite solution, suggested the cruise. Father consented at considerable sacrifice – as he pointed out he hates being away from business – provided she made certain pledges."

"And did she?"

"Of course. She'll hate the cruise – island hopping, sunlight, deck games, people – but to her it's the lesser of two evils."

"Will she keep the pledges, Frances?"

"For a while." She put down her coffee cup. She said, "This could mean disaster. I keep telling myself I should go with them" – she lifted her dark somber eyes –"and so I should, I could . . . well, smooth the surface a little, be a buffer, whatever you want to call it. It wouldn't be the first time. But on their last cruise I didn't go. I was abroad. That was the other time that she –" She broke off, then added flatly,

"The man was a Jamaican. He was the leader of a calypso band at the hotel where they were staying."

"I'm sorry," he said inadequately.

"So was she, presumably. In that case I think he — laughed at her."

Jonathan said, "This is painful for you. Don't go on with it."

"Talking helps."

He asked, "Why does she do it?"

"Drink? . . . Oh, you mean the Jamaican — Kim too, for that matter — and others. . . . I don't know. To humiliate my father, I daresay, and to punish herself." She looked away a moment and then she said, "Sometimes I hope I'll never see her again, and sometimes I'm so sorry for her I could cry — only I don't cry."

The telephone rang and she rose, saying, "I knew this couldn't last."

It didn't.

Driving the considerable distance to the old and pleasant rectory where Henry Stiles lived, Jonathan thought of Maida Lawson and of her daughter. He thought: I can't help Maida Lawson. He could help Frances, mainly by listening. But he had, as it were, no professional standing with her parents.

Dr. Stiles had said on the phone, "It's important that I talk to you, Jonathan, and I'd rather

120

not come to the office."

Arriving, Jonathan found the house blazing with light, and Stiles himself opened the door. He was an unusually attractive man in a dim sort of way – like a carbon copy. Tonight he looked ten or fifteen years older than he was.

It was not the first time that Henry Stiles had consulted Jonathan, other than as a patient – in reference to some difficulty in the parish; a parishioner who must be hospitalized and who hadn't enough money; another with a drinking problem.

They went into the comfortable study: good paintings, a clipper ship beautifully modeled of wood; books, many books; the kind of chairs people relax in so that it becomes easier to talk; the big desk, and on it pictures of Dr. Stiles' late wife and of his children.

"Sit down," said Henry Stiles. He walked over to the fireplace and stood there. "I don't know how to approach this," he admitted.

"Trouble in the parish?"

"No – yes – here," said Dr. Stiles. "Incidentally, when I called your house and spoke to Sophie, I said – I don't know exactly what I said – but the intimation was just that – parish trouble."

"Try sitting down," said Jonathan. "You're not ill are you, Henry?"

It always startled him when he addressed this man by his given name. But he'd known him a long time and the difference in their ages was not much more than a decade.

"No."

Jonathan waited. It occurred to him that he did a good deal of waiting; that was another lonely thing, the waiting. When you could help, when you could do something, and at once, that was different.

Stiles said, "You know Alice."

Yes, Jonathan knew Alice; he also knew Stiles's son Gavin.

"I — I can't bring myself . . ." Stiles cleared his throat. "You'd be astonished," he said, "at how many parents have sat where you are sitting and told me — about their girls — what I have to tell you."

Jonathan said, "All right. You don't have to tell me."

Stiles looked as frightened as if Jonathan had suddenly produced a gun. He said, "You *know?* . . . People *know?*"

"I didn't know," said Jonathan. "As to whether others do or not, I don't know that either. But it's fairly obvious what the problem is . . . Where is she, by the way?"

"Upstairs."

"Do you know who —?"

"I don't," said Stiles violently, "and I don't want to. She's sixteen," he said. "Dear God, she's only sixteen." And it was a cry for help.

"You mean," said Jonathan, "there's no question of marriage?"

"None."

Of course not. Sixteen-year-old daughter of esteemed clergyman, and, one assumed, some local football hero.

"What are we to do?" asked Henry Stiles. He added quickly, "I know you won't do anything?" Yet it was a question, not a statement.

"I won't do anything," said Jonathan evenly, "if you mean what I think you mean. And I don't know anyone who would."

Stiles said helplessly, "I thought – I just thought you might – or could find someone –"

Jonathan said flatly, "I have known of abortionists, or those suspected of performing illegal abortions, Henry. But I would not tell you who they were – or are."

Henry Stiles looked at him through fine, very tired eyes. He said, "Then I don't know what to do."

Jonathan said, "Alice is basically a healthy girl. I recall she didn't turn up at the office for her preschool examination. She's old enough physically to bear a child. If she were eleven . . ." He stopped, then said, "Do you have any relatives, away from here? I mean people who are compassionate and understanding? If so, I'd suggest that she'd be sent to them."

Stiles said, "There is my sister, but she lives in a small town."

"Then," said Jonathan, "there are very good places which will accept a girl in this situation, and see her through, and arrange for the baby's adoption . . . There's one in New York." He stopped and shook his head. "But that," he said, "is too nearby, isn't it? Or Boston?"

Stiles nodded. Many members of his summer congregation came from these cities.

"We can go further afield," Jonathan suggested.

"But what can I say?" asked Stiles helplessly.

"What have you advised other people to say? You have, you know. I remember a discussion much like this one; I made a recommendation as far as the proper place went; you did the rest."

Stiles said heavily, "I said the usual things. I counseled them to say, in the instance of which you speak, that the − the child was ill and being sent to an aunt in another climate."

"You can afford to say you are sending her abroad," said Jonathan.

Stiles said, "Why did this have to happen to me?"

"It happened to Alice," Jonathan reminded him.

"I never thought I'd thank God that my wife didn't live," said Henry Stiles. It wasn't wholly true. Well, he hadn't quite thanked Him, but he had been conscious enough that the celibate life suited him perfectly. "Perhaps if she had," he went on, "this wouldn't have happened."

"Perhaps not, and equally," said Jonathan, "perhaps." He got up, walked around the desk and put his hand on the older man's shoulder. He said, "You have to see her through this, Henry. You have to help her."

"I can't even help myself —"

"You can . . ."

"Oh, prayers," said Stiles with an acid sort of disdain. "What happens when they fail you, when you are asking the impossible? What happens when the God you've always believed stood at your shoulder isn't there?"

"Then," said Jonathan, "I daresay you do what He'd want you to do."

Stiles said, with a thin smile, "Be a man, you mean?"

He believed in his own image, thought Jonathan, he stood in the pulpit and projected it; he brought a great deal to many people . . .

125

he walked on earth as lightly as though he were not a part of it.

He said, "Suppose we talk about arrangements. . . . Say I've discovered Alice doesn't do well in this climate. Actually," he added, frowning slightly, "she was ill twice last year — walking pneumonia and later lobar. Now I'm going to suggest something you won't like. . . ."

"What?"

"Would it be possible for someone to take your place for a few months?"

"My assistant," Stiles said slowly. "He hasn't been here long, of course, but he's well liked." He broke off, and asked, "But the Bishop — what shall I —?"

Jonathan said, "These are matters with which you must deal, Henry. I'll simply recommend that you take Alice to California."

"But —"

"If you let her go alone — and friendless — you'll regret it," Jonathan warned him, "and there appears to be no one who would undertake to be with her. Your sister, I suppose, could not?"

"No. Her family is grown — she's older than I — but has her husband, responsibilities, a house —"

"Also," said Jonathan, "if you send Alice away — or even if you take her and return yourself within a few days – you'll be in a position of not being able to say where she is – exactly. Her friends, yours – they'll want an address. If you go out and stay with her, you can take an apartment and when it is time for her to go into the institution you'll be nearby; you can visit her and – you'll have an address. I must warn you that the place I have in mind, which is from all reports efficient, pleasant and in attractive surroundings is not inexpensive. There are those who cannot, and do not, pay, of course, but for those who are able, the cost is not inconsiderable."

"That doesn't matter!" Henry Stiles looked around his study. "But to leave here!" he said incredulously. "Leave everything!"

"Just for a while."

"But there's Gavin," said Gavin's father. "What am I to tell him?"

Gavin, in college, was a good student. He would enter theological school eventually. He was also charming and – a quality not often associated with charm – sensible.

Jonathan said, "From what I've seen of him, I'd consider Gavin a very steady boy." He thought: And on his way to being considerable man. He added, "It's up to you what you tell him. Personally, I favor the truth. I believe he can take it."

"But what will he do when — we — we are away."

"Stay in college. It would hardly be fair to take him out. You have a housekeeper here; and a great many friends. On vacations a dozen houses will be open to him, including mine, which, I'm afraid, he'd find a little dull. . . . Now, suppose we talk about this California place."

Something less than an hour later, he said, "I'd better see Alice now." Dr. Stiles went to the foot of the curving stairway with him, indicated Alice's room, and then returned to the study, his shoulders stooped. Jonathan went upstairs alone, knocked at a door, and went in to talk to a frightened, wretched girl, his heart wrenched with pity, sorrow, and anger.

Chapter Eight

The dreaming autumn slipped by. There were storms, cold winds, high seas and a great, foaming surf. There were also inevitable colds, accidents on the football field, the ubiquitous virus. In the rectory there was surface normality. Dr. Stiles made two short trips. He went to talk with the Bishop, a wise and quiet gentleman; he went to the university where Gavin was studying. On his return Jonathan stopped to see him and Stiles said, "I didn't – well – evade. Gavin was very shaken, but fine. I don't know how I would have taken it at his age. The Bishop – do you know I used to be a little afraid of him? – he's a powerful man, Jonathan, austere, even. He was most understanding. A – a scandal would be unthinkable, of course."

Alice went to school as usual. She was an integrally self-contained child. One or two remarked that she seemed preoccupied, saw very little of her young friends, went directly home

129

from school and did not have dates, which was curious; she'd always been popular.

The Guild went on and Sophie with it.

Jonathan saw something of Frances. She came by occasionally, saying she needed a breather. Could she take Baffin for a beach run? She had tea with Sophie now and then; she asked her, alone, for dinner; she asked Jonathan and his sister; she asked Jonathan. He found himself looking forward to the evenings, brief as they were, in the guest cottage; and to seeing her in hospital corridors, or running along the beach with Baffin. The season grew, at times somber, with leaden skies and driving rain, or with skies a soft, dove gray and the wind stilled. Frances was like a small flashing light. She appeared to have settled down in Seascape and was going home only for Thanksgiving. After that her parents were leaving on the cruise.

"What about Christmas?" said Sophie.

"I'll hang up my stocking by my own fireplace. It is my own now," she said. "My father gave me the deeds to the cottage and some land."

"You must come to us for Christmas," said Sophie, "not that Jonathan's apt to be home all day."

They were alone, the two women, in the guesthouse.

"I know," said Frances. "Holidays bring on everything from acute indigestion to a rioting appendix."

Before Thanksgiving, Dr. Stiles and his daughter Alice left for California. Her lassitude was now explained, though perhaps not to everyone's satisfaction. But her doctor had prescribed a winter in a milder climate and California, rather than Florida, had been selected. "We have many friends there," Stiles said. It was not the only falsehood he was forced to devise.

"But for heaven's sake," said Sophie, exasperated and frustrated, "What will the parish do without him?"

"It will get along," said Jonathan.

"I daresay. Of course, young Merrow is a very likable and capable man. But he is young."

"You have to start somewhere. He'll make out."

"You don't even know him!"

"Met him recently," said Jonathan. "And his wife. Nice girl."

"Oh, she's all right," said Sophie, "and dedicated to her husband."

"That's wrong?"

"Of course not. But she's pretty earnest about it. And she makes mistakes."

"Naturally."

"People like her," said Sophie. "I'll say that

131

much. Where'd you meet them?"

"At the hospital when Mrs. Beecher was there. I went to see my patient. The Merrows were calling."

"I don't understand about Alice," said Sophie fretfully. "She's always been such a healthy child."

"She was pretty ill last winter," her brother reminded her.

Before the Stiles left there was a party for them in the parish hall, but Alice was not present. Her father explained that, probably because of the excitement, she had been feverish all day.

Sophie said to Henry Stiles, "We'll miss you."

"I'll miss you, too," he said, smiling. She thought he looked ill and wondered if it was not only because of Alice that Jonathan had prescribed this time in the sun. He really should have someone to look after him.

She'd given up her middle-aged dream a while back, or so she thought. Now she found that the dream persisted. She had never considered herself really in love with Henry Stiles. . . . At her age, love? Well, at any age she supposed, if you went along with what you saw and read and heard. But Sophie measured love by her first experience of it. As for other episodes — there had been one or two. She often told her friends that if it hadn't been for Edna's death and Jonathan's situation thereafter, she might have married, which was true. No man had fallen romantically in love with her, perhaps, but what they'd offered had, for a woman such as Sophie, been good, even desirable.

Now looking at Stiles, believing him to be ill, she found herself in a panic of anxiety.

Perhaps he saw it in her eyes. He was not an overly perceptive man where other people were concerned. He waited until they spoke, admitted, confessed, asked for guidance, and then he usually advised them very well.

He asked, "You're worried about something, Sophie?"

"You," she answered with candor.

"About me?" Now it was his turn to feel panic. Not that Sophie Condit wasn't a fine woman; a trifle dominating perhaps, but good, and very useful in the Guild. He admired her. He was quite aware that she — among others — admired him, even indulged in a little hero — or pulpit — worship. He was very perceptive when it came to himself, and to such manifestations. He thought of the Guild, busy with their sewing, their tea giving, their bazaar organizing . . . and of their restless tongues. He had never thought of Sophie as a gossiping woman —

which somewhat set her apart in his mind from a number of parishioners, past and present. Now he thought: She's Jonathan's sister. She is, also, a trained nurse. But no. He had faith in Jonathan Condit . . . he would keep his counsel on any matters concerning patients, friends, strangers.

Watching his expression, Sophie said quickly, "Is something the matter?"

Now she was certain he was ill. Why hadn't Jonathan told her? That was not kind of him. Certainly he was not given to discussion of his patients, but occasionally he did speak of them to her, of his interest and/or anxiety. And Henry was her — their — friend.

He said, "My dear Sophie, nothing's the matter except that, much as I look forward to this trip, I'm distressed at leaving the parish and my friends. Jonathan's a stubborn man. But if it's for Alice's good —"

"Jonathan's usually right," said his sister. "When I said I was worried about you, I mean, you didn't look well. Perhaps you've been over-working? But then you always do. The trip," said Sophie, "should do you as much good as it will Alice."

He looked into her clear eyes and away, ashamed of himself. He was ashamed of himself a good deal of the time now. Is this how a man learns humility? He had always thought of himself as a humble person, esteemed, prosperous, blessed and spared much sorrow — except, of course, he always added hastily, the older Alice's death. He had often, from the pulpit and in his conference study, borne down heavily on two qualities which, he was sure, God approved in His creatures: humility and acceptance.

He said to Sophie, "I hope it will do us both good."

He was a man without much humor; he had enough to get by, of course, and he'd cultivated it painstakingly. Now not for the first time in the past weeks he was experiencing a sort of sea change, a trend toward irony.

Sophie came steaming home at a fairly late hour and saw Jonathan's light shining under the door. She rapped smartly and came in, a handsome woman, slightly flushed, and wearing, as he had observed at dinner, her most becoming frock.

"Have a good time?" he inquired, putting his book aside. It was one Frances had suggested that he read. He didn't like it; its clinical sex bored him. However, it was, he conceded, an honest book, and he admired honesty.

Sophie sat down. She said, "Everyone

was there, everyone —"

"I daresay. How about the food?"

"The girls outdid themselves," reported Sophie, pokerfaced. "There was even a mild species of punch — and something without punch for the stricter among us."

There were times when Sophie exerted herself to be amusing; Jonathan had learned to be wary of such occurrences.

"Everyone is unhappy, of course, that Henry's going away."

"My dear Sophie, he hasn't been transferred to Malaysia!"

"I know, but you get used to a person." She leaned forward and said urgently, "Jonathan, will you answer a question — truthfully?"

"If I can," he said cautiously.

"Is Henry ill? I mean is that why you're sending him to California?"

He said, "I'm sending Alice. No, Henry isn't ill. He's somewhat alarmed about the kid, of course — although he needn't be — and he doesn't want to leave any more than you want him to." He did not emphasize the pronoun, but she looked at him quickly.

She rose and said, "Well, I'll leave you to your book." She glanced at the title and made a little face. "Isn't that the one —?"

"It is."

136

"Well, for heaven's sake! I never thought you'd find time for trash!"

"It's not trash. It isn't pleasant and what it calls a spade wouldn't have been fit to print a few years ago. But it's well written. And I'm sure you'll think more highly of it when I tell you Frances asked me to read it."

Sophie went out, closing the door a little harder than was necessary.

The Stiles, father and daughter, departed. Frances went home for an unfestive Thanksgiving; too much food; numerous relatives, most of them dull; a couple of Maida's unattached young men; her husband glowering at the head of the vast silver- and crystal-laden table; and Maida as if with malice aforethought, ostentatiously sober, and saying so to anyone who cared to listen.

"By way of giving thanks," she explained, "for my many blessings, I am at the moment off the sauce." She added thoughtfully that it was not the happiest of situations.

During the next weeks the weather held to daytime sun and, on the little ponds, nightfall freeze. The trees had relinquished color and leaves; only the pines were green. There was as yet very little snow, only an occasional lazy down-drifting which did not remain on the roads. But early mornings there would be ice, and there were the usual accidents . . .

"You drive too fast," Jonathan told Frances one day, as he saw her pull into the hospital parking space.

"I know."

"Well, don't," he suggested reasonably. "I've enough trouble without adding you to my emergencies."

They had, he thought, settled into a good, give-and-take friendship. He liked to listen to her; he liked her listening to him. There'd been no further — what would you call them? — candid advances on her part. Having spoken her piece once, she appeared to rest her case.

It had been a long time since he'd had such a pleasant understanding relationship with a woman. A long time? All his life, unless you counted his mother, and that, of course, was a different matter. He'd never enjoyed it with Sophie. As for Edna, he had loved her with tenderness and with passion, but they had not had time, before her death, to grow up together, to grow into friendship as well as love.

He said to Frances, one cold evening when she had stopped by to bring Sophie a birthday gift, "I've enjoyed knowing you."

"Well, thanks." He'd walked out to her car with her and stood bareheaded with ice-cold

138

moonlight on her silver-gold hair. "That's a quaint thing to say, also nice. To coin a cliché, no one really knows anyone."

"True enough," said Jonathan, "in a general way. Shall I rephrase it? I've enjoyed knowing you as much as I now know you."

"Are you going off to be a medical missionary?" she inquired not without alarm. "You keep putting it in the past."

"I'm staying at my post here," he said, laughing, "and I was referring to the immediate past. By the way, what happened to Kim Sylvester? I haven't seen him around lately."

"Oh, he went off to join some people on a yacht – a cruise I believe – where you go as a guest but behave like the crew – of which you're expected to be part."

"I can't imagine him in that role."

"You underestimate him," she said. "He sails, boxes, plays good tennis, and swims like an otter or something. I didn't believe you'd be fooled by the deliberate image he projects."

"I wasn't," said Jonathan, with a vision of Sylvester in a galley or swarming up a mast. "Get in your car, woman, you'll catch cold."

"I never catch cold, Doctor."

Sophie was pleased with her gift; an antique pin, small but with considerable charm. She said, when Jonathan came back into the house,

139

"I'm glad you understand Frances better than you did."

"Perhaps I do."

"And," said Sophie firmly, for she liked to dot her i's and cross her t's ". . . like her better."

"That too," he agreed, "but don't build up false hopes."

He crooked a finger at Baffin, murmured, "Exit laughing," and started for his office. He had appointments coming up.

Sophie said, "Wait a minute. You've had several letters from Henry lately."

Jonathan stood still. Of course, Sophie sorted the mail. He knew her well enough, however, to know that she would open nothing of his, and Henry's letters were all marked personal.

They were painful and revealing reports on what he now knew of the so-called Home; of the apartment he'd found after several days in a hotel; of Alice. "I'm trying to draw closer to her; it isn't easy . . ." And in another letter: "If only she would confide in me. But I believe she is glad I'm here." In still another, he wrote: "I am continually wondering how much I was to blame. I have always been very busy, but there was time for the children, I thought. . . . I brought them up to the best of my ability."

He spoke, too, of Gavin; of the letters he'd had from him; of the carefully careless scrawls that Alice now and then received from her brother. And he said, "I'm teaching her myself; there's no need for a tutor. We brought her textbooks out; the work had been outlined for her. I find it passes my time as well as hers and that I am a rather good teacher. She says so, anyway."

Jonathan answered Sophie. He said, "Yes, he writes me. I've recommended a doctor out there – I don't know him personally, but I looked him up – and Henry keeps me informed of Alice's general health. But," he added, "you've heard from him, too, haven't you?"

"Oh, one note," she said, "giving the address and all."

He thought: No, she wouldn't open my mail, and I don't believe she'd read it, even if it sat looking at her on the desk. Nevertheless, I'm glad I destroyed the letters as soon as I'd read 'em.

He answered Henry's letters; for a physician Jonathan wrote a remarkably clear hand. He urged him not to press Alice for her confidence. "She was open with me to a degree," he had written, "as I told you after I'd talked with her. But no name was mentioned, of course. You know that. Henry, don't urge, don't prod, don't pry. She's going to be even more frightened than she is now as time goes on. Prepare

141

yourself for that. You can help her."

He usually mailed these letters himself instead of leaving them in the basket on his desk for Sophie to mail when she went to the village on errands. He also began stopping by the post office for their mail. When she commented on that, he said, "I was going by, thought I'd save you a trip." Then he decided that it was simpler to open the box, extract the letter from Henry if one was there, and leave the rest of the mail in the box untouched. The performance began to feel uncommonly like a sort of intrigue and he didn't like it.

Frances spoke of Dr. Stiles once, when she came to have tea with Sophie. Jonathan and Baffin wandered in while they were discussing the rector.

"I'm sorry Alice is ill," said Frances. "I've seen her a time or two. I don't specially like Henry Stiles by the way, but his son's a living doll. I ran into him at the outdoor art show last summer. He had good taste and pronounced rather astute opinions, I thought."

"Why don't you like Henry Stiles?" asked Sophie.

Frances thought: Oh, dear! I should have remembered. . . . She got around, she heard a thing or two. But she answered truthfully, "No special reason. I'm not a member of his congre-

142

gation; I hardly know him. He's attractive enough, he has a good voice. . . . Oh, yes," she said in answer to Jonathan's look of unbelief, "I went to his church once. Sat in the back, slipped out during the handshaking. . . . Yes," she went on reflectively, "a good voice, though I have never cared for what I call the trained ecclesiastical voice, sonorous rise and fall." She laughed. "I'm no judge. The only clergyman I ever liked was the one who married me to Charles — which was not his fault, poor dear. He talked to you from the pulpit as if he were talking to you in your living room. As for the sermon I heard Dr. Stiles deliver, that was all right, too, but — like the man himself — a little too spiritual."

"Too spiritual!" cried Sophie, roused to horror. "How can you say that?"

"Quite easily. When sermons get too spiritual, they lack punch. On the other hand, when they cease to be sermons and become, as they often do, passionate politics or causes — that's worse."

Jonathan said, "You're something of a brat."

"Oh," said Frances cheerfully, "I know how everyone goes on about Dr. Stiles. I just don't go along with it. The boy told me he's going into the ministry, too. I bet he'll cause a fluttering in the dovecotes. It's no wonder that

143

clergymen and doctors marry young," she said with a wicked glance at her host. "For self-protection, I suppose – not that it always works."

"Well," said Jonathan, "all very interesting, but I've got to go out and see a woman you both know who has five children – all without benefit of clergy."

They knew her. Everyone knew her. She lived on the fringes of the village, worked hard, dragged up her children with a strong but loving hand, was beholden to no one, asked no charity in the literal or any other sense, took in washing and was not at all ashamed of her past peccadilloes. She'd explain them if you asked her – and a lot of people, mainly women, had. . . . One of the gentlemen was married and she didn't want to break up his home, despite the fact his wife was a first-class bitch. The other one died before he could marry her. He'd promised, but kept putting it off. She was sure he would have gotten round to it in time if the good Lord had spared him.

"What's wrong with our Unwed Matron," inquired Frances, who, with, or without, laundry, often stopped by the falling-down but spotlessly clean cottage.

"Flu," said Jonathan. "I'll have to find someone to keep an eye on the two youngest kids."

"If you get stuck for a mother's helper," said Frances, "I'm available. . . . What do you want for Christmas?"

"Peace and quiet," said Jonathan.

Frances thought, going home: Well I try, don't I?. . . . Volunteer at the hospital, elegant cook in a kitchenette, sympathetic listener, and now, baby sitter. I'd make a darned good wife she told herself, especially a doctor's wife. I must admit "volunteering" may have begun with something of a motive, but now I like it. Even if he weren't in the picture, I'd like it.

She thought ahead to spending Christmas with Sophie and Jonathan and smiled. Gavin Stiles would be there for dinner, too. Jonathan had written to ask him. She could do without Gavin and Sophie, but half a loaf was still nourishing.

Chapter Nine

On Christmas Eve, Jonathan spent several hours at the hospital with a seriously ill patient. There was a long consultation. He had soup and a sandwich in the coffee shop, and later, when he could afford to be absent a few minutes, he looked in on Mary Karlin, who was physically doing very well. Her mother was with her; a fat, red stocking hung from the foot of the bed. Sam Karlin wasn't there.

Jonathan asked Mrs. Karlin where he was and she said he had to work — something to do with the books before the first of the year.

Jonathan sat a moment beside Mary and talked to her quietly, and she answered him. She was lucid and not in much pain, but her eyes, he thought, no longer belonged to her. They were the eyes of a stranger, reluctant to look out upon a confusing and inexplicable world.

The hospital was gay with wreaths; there was a big tree in the downstairs lobby, smaller ones in the waiting rooms on every corridor; there were carols and bells and cheerful faces — and sick people, anxious to go home — or too ill to care.

Barring emergencies, there would be no patients at the office tonight and Jonathan would, therefore, be free. When he left his patient, confident that his situation had greatly bettered, he stopped, as he'd promised he would, at Frances'. Sophie was to be there and a few others for an informal celebration.

Half a dozen in all; a little tree, packages, and, as Frances had announced, her stocking hung from the fireplace mantel.

"Santa Claus?" Jonathan asked.

"Sometimes," said Frances, "you have to be your own."

She served a simple buffet, and the small bar was stocked; one of the laundress's girls was there to help. Named for her mother, Clarissa Dorothea, she was the oldest of the children, intelligent, rather pretty, and in high school.

"How'd you ever get anyone on Christmas Eve?" Jonathan asked Frances and she said, "Well, a buck's a buck, and young Clarissa is saving to go to college."

Clarissa was in the kitchen, so he wondered aloud: "I don't know her, of course, except as an occasional patient. If anyone in the family makes college she will — not, I think the two boys, or the smaller girls. It would be interesting to know what their relationship with their mother is —"

"Good," said Frances. "Have you forgotten I spent the better part of three days there — and didn't catch the flu? The kids are crazy about their happy, feckless mama. The boys go about cordially smacking anyone in the puss who dares say an unkind word about her. I understand they've fought their way up from elementary school and are greatly respected by their fellow students. As for Clarissa, Jr., she knows the score and while she bears no animosity toward her mother, she'll be careful, I think, not to follow her rather — well — generous example."

Once during the evening Jonathan, taking a tray to the kitchen, found himself alone with Clarissa Dorothea. He said, "I'm afraid you're missing the family festivities."

"They'll all be up when I get home," she told him. "We've a tree and everything, and a big turkey for tomorrow with all the trimmings."

Frances, he thought.

Before he left, he looked over his small change, found a shiny new quarter, took a pen and wrote "For a good girl" on a prescription blank and when no one was looking popped it

148

into the top of Frances' stocking.

Baffin, comforted with sundry delicacies, had taken up his own familiar station by the fireplace. Conversation was easy and pleasant. Jonathan and Sophie knew Frances' other guests, a childless couple from the other side of town and one of the high-school teachers, a young man new to the community. The party ended early, as parties go, and Jonathan said, "Sophie can go home alone. I'll wait and take Clarissa."

"I expected to," said Frances.

"There's been a little glaze of ice since sundown," he told her, "and there's apt to be some pretty wild driving."

So everyone left except Jonathan and Baffin, and Clarissa whistling, on an accurate key, one of the familiar carols, washed up and set things away.

"Tell me what you put in your stocking," said Jonathan.

"Frivolities. I've never had a stocking, you know."

He hadn't, since he was a child, he admitted. "But," he said, "there's no element of surprise, when you do it yourself?"

"You're mistaken, sometimes I surprise myself." She added that her friends in the city had sent packages; some were small enough to go into the stockings. The parental check, also, she said, "But, that's in my desk."

"I haven't really thanked you for helping out with Clarissa's family," Jonathan said.

"I enjoyed it," she said honestly. "It was a complete madhouse, clean enough, although the house looked as if it had been stirred with an eggbeater. The kids are remarkably courteous as well as noisy. And there was nothing to do for the stricken mama but straighten sheets, administer medicine, fetch trays and bedpans, and give baths. As a matter of fact the junior Clarissa did the harder work."

She added casually that friends had written to ask if she'd take a trip with them, later in the year — another one of the cruises.

"Will you?"

"I'm thinking about it. I'd be gone only about three weeks. Of course the parents won't like it. They'll say if I can go on a cruise, why didn't I go with them?"

He said, "It might be good for you, Frances. Perhaps you need the change."

"I'll consider it. Will you miss me?"

"Yes," he said truthfully.

"Then I think I'll go — good discipline for you," she said, laughing.

Clarissa looked into the living room and reported she'd be ready in a minute. Baffin rose from lovely dreams of long exciting swims and shook himself. As Jonathan walked toward the door, Frances caught up with him, pointed to the mistletoe descending from the lintel, drew his tall head down and kissed him briefly if not lightly. "Merry Christmas," she said, although everyone had said it at midnight. "See you tomorrow."

Driving Clarissa home, Jonathan asked her about her school work, and added that he understood she wanted to go to college.

"Oh, I do," she told him, "and I've applied" — she told him where — "and been accepted. I've worked for a thousand years," she added, "after school, holidays, and summers. I've the money saved for books and clothes and board — and it's a state college. But I don't know how Mom will manage without me. Maybe I shouldn't go. Maybe I ought to get a job here after graduation and help out."

"What does your mother say?"

"She says it's my life," Clarissa told him. "She says that's all you can be sure of until it ends for good — that your life's your own and you do with it what you want to do. . . . I suppose she means according to your limitations," she ended soberly.

When they reached her house, Clarissa said, "Please come in for a minute.

151

Mom'd be so pleased."

So he went in . . . and the tree was lighted, a radio was going, and there were packages all about, some opened and some not, and the elder Clarissa had on an astonishing old dressing gown given her, he judged, by one of her clients. The children were swarming like bees, the noise was deafening, and Seascape's most outstanding example of live and let live and be damned to you was sitting in a platform rocker in the middle of the room, oblivious of the noise, stroking a brushed-wool sweater.

Everyone shouted greetings, and his hostess said amiably, "Glad you could come, Doctor." She waved a hand about the room. "Looks a mess," she said cheerfully, "but the kids are having the time of their lives. Mrs. Lawson"— she indicated the packages – "she certainly went to town. You know she did a fine job of looking after things until Clary got home from school, up to when I got back on my feet."

Jonathan said, yes he knew.

"Good as gold that one," she said. "Gave me this sweater and some perfume."

She reeked of it.

Jonathan admired all the presents and then took his departure, and when he reached home Sophie, appearing at the head of the stairs, remarked that he'd taken his time.

"Took young Clarissa home," he said, "and looked in on the excitement."

"Her mother's an exception to the rule of them that has gets. I understand people in town have been doing for her for years," Sophie commented.

"Also," he said, "she does for herself. She works, and hard."

"Well," she said, "get to bed. Tomorrow's another day, and Mrs. Parker will be here practically at dawn."

"I offered her the day off," said Jonathan. "We could have managed without her. I told you we could have had the turkey cooked at the rotisserie."

Sophie shrugged. She said, "Mrs. P. doesn't mind and she's paid extra. What has she to go home to, anyway?"

Which was true enough.

Jonathan and Baffin yawned their way upstairs. Baffin had had a brief run in the crisp air and was sleepy again. And Sophie asked, "Nice party, wasn't it?"

"Very."

"Frances tell you she might go off on a trip?"

Sophie muttered something which sounded like, "There's a limit to patience," but he purposely didn't hear it. He went to bed and lay thinking awhile, his arms crossed behind his

153

head. A kiss beneath the mistletoe can be pleasant, meaningless or disturbing. He thought: I don't want to be involved, and yet he realized he had been drifting for some time toward just that.

Young Gavin Stiles came for dinner; he was staying with friends over vacation, and going to parties; he'd been up late the night before. And Jonathan said, "You're kind to come to us, Gavin, I'm sure you had many invitations and the Schmidts must be celebrating."

They were his hosts. They'd had their big party last night. It was a good one, Gavin reported.

He was a handsome boy; he looked like his father but the top copy rather than the carbon.

He added, "I wanted to come here, I really wanted to."

He looked at Frances in her cranberry-red dress, with little golden bells in her ears. They tinkled as she moved. He had met her only at that outdoor art show. He thought she looked, today, like a sophisticated angel.

Jonathan watched him during the time they spent together and saw how his eyes followed Frances and how he colored when she spoke to him, and thought: How painful — how wonderful — how heartbreaking — to be young.

After dinner, which, Jonathan conceded, wasn't too bad, they opened the presents; there were gifts for Gavin, too. And Frances opened first her gift from Sophie, which was handkerchiefs, and then the one from Jonathan . . . which together with Sophie's and Mrs. Parker's he'd rushed into a shop, bought and rushed out. Frances' was one of those intricate wallet purses which women like, a place for everything. And she looked up and said, "I've something to keep in it, too," reaching in her handbag, removed a new quarter and put it in. "There," she said with satisfaction.

Baffin had given her a present: a ball-point pen. She went down on her knees beside him on the floor and hugged him hard. Baffin said, thanks, and moved a little away. He liked her and the way she smelled, the manner in which she scratched behind his ears, and the pleasant company she provided on the beach. But he was not given to hugging back.

"When I go away," said Frances, "I'll write you often."

Baffin nodded; he was sure she would.

Before Gavin left he asked if he could speak to Jonathan and Jonathan took him in the office and shut the door.

"Shoot," he said.

"I'd sure like to."

"I'm sure you would, but in the first place you don't know whom to shoot."

"I think I do."

"Then keep it to yourself; and shooting's no solution."

Gavin said, "I'm so darned sorry for Alice — and my father."

"Yes, I know."

"I wish I knew why . . ."

Not why he was sorry, but why he had come to sorrow and by what path.

Jonathan said carefully, "Perhaps she was lonely."

"But she was always so popular."

"Always?"

"Well, not exactly . . . In the last year or so —" He broke off and asked, *"That?"*

"Sometimes just that, sometimes the longing to be popular. It's one standard, Gavin; not a high one but still a standard."

Gavin said, "If there were only something I could do."

He'd grown up, these last months; not that he hadn't been maturing normally, but the steadiness had increased, and the gravity.

"There's nothing but — I daresay this will sound corny to you — love, Gavin. For Alice, for your father."

"It doesn't sound corny," said Gavin. "And it

didn't when He said it."

He left after a while and Frances asked him to come by and see her before he returned to the university. "Phone first," she suggested. "I have odd hours at the hospital."

"Gosh, thanks, Mrs. Lawson," said Gavin.

Frances stayed on after Mrs. Parker had left. Later they'd have a scratch supper, every man for himself.

"Best Christmas I ever had," said Frances, flat on the old living-room couch. "You ought to have attended some of ours. For your sins. Relatives. Parties, thousands of presents, boredom. And as for those parties Charles and I gave" — she paused — "very unsuccessful unless at least two of our guests passed out cold."

They had a late supper, cold turkey, cranberry sauce, Sophie's really good salad and the rest of the Christmas wine, and Frances helped Sophie wash up while Jonathan went upstairs to look, half asleep, at television. When he came down, Frances was demanding, "Where is that lout? I have to go home."

The telephone rang and Jonathan, after answering and hanging up, said sadly, "And I can't stay home."

So they went out together, he with Baffin to the old car and Frances to the little coupé she had given herself earlier in the season.

She didn't think a canary-colored convertible was compatible with winter.

It was starting to snow, the stars were veiled and the snow a quiet, feathery fall.

"Drive carefully," he admonished.

"I shall. Good night, Jon, and thank you for everything."

She went out ahead of him, turned off, beeped twice on her horn and he drove, smiling a little, toward the house of a little boy who had had far too much Christmas, and was also coming down with measles.

Frances drove carefully. The snow was now fairly thick over the skim of ice. Other people didn't drive as carefully. . . . She tried to get out of the way and succeeded, by slamming into a tree beside the country road. The other car went on.

She was out for a few moments and when she came back to a quiet world of snow, the air was blowing bitter cold through shattered glass. She said something short, sharp, and — she felt — appropriate, and decided that she wasn't dead. Her head hurt and she was bleeding from a gash across one instep, a cut on her face. Otherwise she seemed to be in one piece.

She tried to start the car and, failing, got out and walked through the snow to the nearest house. The owners had gone to bed, but presently someone opened the door and said mildly, "Thought I heard a crash."

"May I use your phone?" asked Frances, faintly.

The man — and he was quite old — caught her and eased her into a chair. "Mother," he yelled, and Frances thought dizzily: If he has a mother, she must be a hundred years old. He went himself to the phone where presently he was shouting brief recommendations to the police department.

Mother came downstairs, fat and comfortable and wrapped in various warm garments. And Father went into the kitchen and returned with a glass of brandy. "Warms you up," he said.

Mother said, "You know better than that. Could be something's wrong with her head. Who's your doctor?"

"Doctor Condit," said Frances.

"Jon," said Mother, pleased. She introduced herself and Frances said, "I'm Frances Lawson."

"Over to Driftwood," said Mother. "Father worked on the trees there when you was building. . . . Don't get up. Set."

She called the Condit house and Sophie answered.

Presently Mother reported. "Jon's sister says she knows where to get him; she says you stay right here with us."

"But —"

"Better keep quiet," said Father, abstractedly drinking the "warmer upper," and putting a shovelful of coal on the hearth fire.

Frances stayed. Her face stung and her ankle. Certainly it couldn't be just the cut. She remembered, then, she had turned it, and fallen, just as she reached the steps of the little house.

The police came. There were consultations. No, she hadn't seen the license of the other car — or noted the make or color; it had just loomed up ahead of her, full, she thought hazily of young people.

"What else?" said the officer gloomily.

They towed her car away; no station would be open tonight. Where'd she trade? She told them, and they'd no more than departed, after making cryptic notes, than Jonathan came.

He banged on the door and Father shouted that it was open. "Hi, Jon," said Father, whose given name proved to be Horace, "look what Santa Claus left us. She ain't hurt bad, I don't think."

Jonathan said severely, "I told you to drive carefully."

"Damn it, I did!" she said, roused to fury, and Mother made clucking noises.

Jonathan commandeered the downstairs spare

160

room. It was colder than the top of Mt. Everest, but it served.

The cuts were not deep; they were soon taken care of; the ankle, however, was swelling.

So with good-byes and good lucks and thanks for everything, Frances left. Jonathan carried her out to his car and Baffin wuffed crossly, "For heavens sakes, what next?"

Jonathan got into the car remarking, "Well, not much damage."

"I'll be scarred?" she asked.

"Of course not, idiot. You won't be able to get about much on that foot. No break, but we'll X-ray anyway — so I'm taking you home with me."

"Kathleen," said Frances obscurely.

"What's that?"

"Nothing. I was once in love with an Irish tenor."

Jonathan said, "Maybe you have a concussion, after all."

So he took her back to his house. Sophie was up and Jonathan carried Frances upstairs and into the spare room, which wasn't as cold as Mother and Father's, and left her to his sister's skillful ministrations.

Temperature? None. Some shock, yes. Superficial cuts, bruises from the fall, and a sprained ankle. "Tomorrow the works,"

161

said Jonathan, "just to be sure."

He was leaving the room when Frances said querulously, "All my presents, in the car . . . everything –"

"They'll keep."

"And the lights on in the guesthouse."

"You can afford it."

"I did remember to turn off the tree lights," she said.

"Good," said Jonathan, and added, " 'Night."

Chapter Ten

Frances remained at the Condit house over New Year's. The cuts healed, there were no bones broken in the ankle. Jonathan borrowed a crutch for her. "Something I've always wanted!" said Frances. And Sophie had gone to the guesthouse the day after Christmas to turn off the lights and pack a bag for her unexpected guest. Sophie couldn't have been happier with the situation. They'll see each other every day, she thought, planning to visit her friends evenings, or turn up at Guild meetings, or whatever. The enforced proximity of her brother and Frances Lawson took Sophie's restless mind at least temporarily from her own problem: Why had Henry Stiles really gone to California? Was Jonathan concealing something from her? When would Henry return?

Frances spent her days reading, writing letters, and permitting the curious quietude of the house to sink into her bones. Outwardly it was not quiet; patients came and went, Mrs. Parker crashed about the kitchen, the telephone incessantly rang, and Sophie's was not a serene personality. Yet there was a serenity within these walls. She said so to Jonathan once. "Nice people have lived here," she remarked and, he agreed, "Certainly, for a great many years — summers anyway — the Condits."

"I don't mean your family. I don't even mean you; but before the Condits ever set foot in Seascape. Houses have definite personalities. I think they draw upon those who have lived in them."

"You could be right," he conceded, thinking, for the first time of the homes into which he had walked as guest or physician, and of the fact that in some he felt restless, or at least unquiet, and in others — even if the situation was professionally serious — oddly at peace.

They celebrated New Year's Eve, together with some some friends of Sophie's, at the Condit house. Jonathan was out until just before midnight; later he was called out again and didn't reappear until breakfast. People were celebrating in their own seventy-five-m.p.h. fashion, and this meant emergencies, ambulances, doctors, surgeons.

Young Gavin came in New Year's afternoon. Jonathan was busy, Sophie was out, so Gavin sat and talked to Frances.

Later she remarked, "That boy has something on his mind."

"The thoughts of youth —" Jonathan began and Frances said, "Skip it. I mean, he's troubled."

"Marks," deduced Sophie briskly.

"I don't think so. Perhaps he's beginning to wonder of he's selected the right profession."

"Could be," said Jonathan. "Most of us have some misgivings. I know I did, pre-med."

"Anyway," said Frances firmly, "it's as if he carried a burden."

"Oh," said Sophie, "I daresay he misses his father and sister. It's not easy to spend holidays in someone else's house, but it would have been twice as bad if he'd come home to his own, although there's someone to look after him." She paused and said to Jonathan, "I didn't think of it before, but I wonder why he didn't fly out to California for his vacation."

"Costs considerable," Jonathan reminded her.

"Oh," said Sophie, "that wouldn't be of any consequence. Henry has money of his own, you know, which he inherited; and Gavin, as well as Henry and Alice, inherited from Mrs. Stiles."

Frances, watching Jonathan without appearing to, saw a shadow cross his eyes, and thought, There's something wrong and Jon knows, but he isn't telling. She bet herself her shining new quarter that Sophie wouldn't find out. She'd learned a good deal in these past days about Jonathan and his sister.

In the new year, which was cold and which now and then decided to snow, she went back to the guesthouse. The crutch was returned whence it came, and she used a cane. One of Jonathan's father's, which he had cut down for her. And she said, when he took her home, "I've decided to go on the cruise."

"When?"

"Early next month. I'll be able to get about, with only an interesting limp."

"Not even that if you don't overdo. It will do you good," he said, "You've been restive, I think, shut up in the house, not getting to the hospital, just living in a dull secure fashion with the Condits."

"Oddly enough," she said, "I like things — dull; not that they were. But I think perhaps I'd better shake the sand of Seascape off my feet for a little while. It will give me time to think."

"About what?" he inquired and instantly regretted it.

"Myself . . . you. . . ."

They were alone in the guesthouse. The heat had been left on, someone had come to clean, and it looked as if it had never been deserted.

She said, "Propinquity is — well, like the

glaze of ice I hit Christmas evening. With me, it affords no threat. I just liked it, of course. But for you . . ."

True enough, he thought; seeing her every day, talking, laughing or finding out, as he had, that there can be communication between two people without a word spoken, had been, and was, disturbing.

She said lightly, "So I'll go away for a while and give you time to ponder. I'm not staying on here, Jon. I'll call the house tonight and McKenzie can drive up for me. I'll leave the car in the garage. I won't need it in town."

He said, "I'll miss you."

"That's good." She was sitting in a big chair, her slender foot on a stool. "Come here," she said. "Kiss me good-by — and properly — just for luck."

"Good or bad, and whose?"

"Who knows?"

He kissed her and enjoyed it, and then she said, "Now, go away."

He did so thoughtfully. He hadn't wished to be involved seriously, emotionally; and he was becoming so. His heart saluted her; she was giving him a way out — for a time at least; enough time to regain balance and return to the old, casual relationship.

Sophie went into something of a snit when he

told her of Frances' plans. She said indignantly, "She didn't tell me she'd made up her mind to go."

"Maybe if she hadn't had the accident, she wouldn't have decided to," said Jonathan. "At any rate, it will be fine for her."

Sophie had a house full of flowers and a letter of gratitude from her departed guest. "I'll come back," Frances wrote, "after my little laze in the sun. I've promised the hospital, and I promise you."

"Disappointed?" asked Jonathan, over coffee at dinner.

"Of course," said Sophie.

"Like the song," he suggested, "you've grown accustomed to her face."

"I thought maybe you would."

"I did," he said soberly. "Nice face, too, under all the glop."

"Not much glop as you put it, and anyway how do you know?"

"I saw her with it freshly washed a time or two," said Jonathan, and rose. He had office hours. "Poor Sophie," he said, smiling.

"Poor you," said Sophie tartly.

"Yes, I know," he said standing beside her chair, "but did it ever occur to you that I might not want to remarry?"

She said, "That's nonsense. Edna's been gone

a long time. You're young; you need a wife and a family."

"Possibly. But not yet."

In February after Frances had sailed, Sam Karlin came without appointment to the office, completely distraught. Office hours had not yet started. Sophie and Jonathan were at dinner. Mrs. Parker announced briefly, "Sam Karlin's here. You'd better see him, Doctor."

Jonathan said. "Show him into the office."

"For heaven's sake," said Sophie, "if you can't even have a meal . . ."

He rose and went into the office. Karlin was standing looking from the windows. He wore his overcoat, his cap was in his hands, wrung between them.

Jonathan said, "Take off your coat, Sam, and sit down. What's wrong?"

It couldn't be Mary. The hospital would have called him. She was not due to come home again for a while.

"It's my wife," said Karlin, "and Olive —"

"Olive?" Jonathan thought, but she was pledged not to continue haunting the Karlin house. She had said so; Susan had said so.

"It didn't mean anything," Karlin said savagely. "I've been half out of my head with worry. . . . Mary and what happened and then money. It's cost a fortune. I'd mortgaged the house. We hadn't hardly paid it off. But I mortgaged it again. I'm into the bank up to my neck. And she – my wife – she was living at the hospital practically. A man gets lonesome. I took Olive out, a few times. Her aunt didn't want her coming to the house no more. So I'd take her out when my wife was at the hospital; we'd have dinner, I'd drop her off and go on to see Mary. Folks saw us –" He broke off. Then, "Doc, for God's sake I had to have someone to talk to – you understand that?"

"Yes."

"Then Doctor Marod said that Mary – once she's able – has got to be sent away somewhere."

"Let's not put it like that. She must have treatment, I know. I've talked to Doctor Marod. You've had it explained to you. Where Doctor Marod proposes to place her there'll be very little expense, nothing beyond her personal needs."

"That's charity!"

"You can't have it both ways, Sam. Either you pay, or you accept state care. It's a good place. Fine doctors and nurses; and she'll be helped. Because of her physical illness, Doctor Marod hasn't been able to do very much with her. But he and his colleagues probably can, once she is healed and on her feet."

"My wife's dead set against it," said Karlin. "She says nothing's wrong with Mary except the burns; she says she can take care of her; she says it's me — that I want her out of the way because of Olive. And she's written to the School Board."

"Do you know what she wrote?"

"No, but it's not hard to figure."

"Would she let me talk to her?"

"I don't think so. She says it's all your fault."

"Mine!"

"Doctor Marod — everything — encouraging Susan Jarvis to work in the store and Olive to help around the house;"

Jonathan said, "This will be rough on Olive and Susan. Perhaps they'll come to me. I can talk to members of the Board. I know them all."

"I know 'em too," said Sam, "but it won't do any good. You know what this town is like. The parents hear things; they get upset — as if there weren't enough going on among their own children." He rose. He said, "I had to tell you, Doc."

Jonathan unlocked a cabinet and took out a square bottle, shook some tablets into an envelope and wrote on it. He said, "Suppose you take these — as directed."

"What for?"

"Nothing harmful. Just something to

171

calm you down a little."

He said, "Well, O.K., thanks. But I hate like hell going back to that house, with her yelling at me and everything."

"I'm sure you do. I would, too. But you can't stay away forever, and you have great responsibility. Mary, for one, and Olive for another. For Olive *is* your responsibility. You're a grown man and considerably older than Olive. Being lonely isn't a valid excuse. Are you in love with her?"

"Hell, no," said Sam, astonished. "I haven't been in love for years. I just like to talk to her. She listens."

He went out and Jonathan thought: Well, that's a warning; loneliness, and the need for a listener.

He got into his car after office hours, and went to the Jarvis house. Susan opened the door. She looked as if someone had beaten her, even if the bruises didn't show.

"May I come in, Susan? Sam Karlin's been to see me."

"Come in." She took him into the kitchen and said, "Olive's locked up in her room. She has to see the Board tomorrow."

"So Mrs. Karlin did write?"

"She wrote, she phoned, she's talked all over town," said Susan, white. "The girl's been a fool, Jon" – he noticed that for the first time in years she called him that – "and Sam Karlin's another. I wouldn't expect Olive to have much sense after what happened back at home. But Sam –"

He said, "Take it easy, Susan. I'm sure that there's nothing which can't be set straight."

"If you mean, has she been . . . I know she hasn't. That isn't her trouble," said Susan. "Her trouble is liking men she believes need her; men she can – well – manage; men she thinks she can help."

He said, "Ask her if she'll see me."

Susan went wearily upstairs and presently returned. She said, "No, if you don't mind, not tonight. She's been crying her eyes out."

For the second time that evening he produced, this time from his bag, a mild sedative, an envelope, a pen. "You make her take these," he said, "and you could do with one yourself."

"I don't need medicine," said Susan firmly.

He said. "Well, call me if you need me," and went back to Baffin and the car. Oh, my dear God, he thought, driving off. *People!*

It took a while for the Board to decide . . . and their decision was that indiscretion is not a desirable quality in a teacher. Jonathan did some conferring to some effect, and Olive

Evans was permitted to resign.

So Olive was in her aunt's house with no place to go. There was no question of returning to the store. And there were few other positions open in town at this time of year.

She came to see Jonathan. She said, "I could go home, I suppose." She was very thin, and her eyes, her pretty eyes, were dulled. "But . . . I don't know. Maybe they wouldn't have me. And then there's Aunt Susan. I don't want to leave her. But I'd like to get away from this town and all the talk and —" She broke off, then said helplessly, "I don't know what to do."

Jonathan was reminded of Henry Stiles and of a hundred other patients. They always said helplessly, "I don't know what to do," or, "I don't know where to go," or, "I don't know where to turn."

People. God help them.

He said, "Stick it out, Olive. We'll find something for you somehow. Can you type?"

"Why yes," she said, "I took a course. I'm not an expert. I've forgotten most of the shorthand I once knew — but I can type. I'm slow, but careful."

She was anything but that, he thought. Aloud he said, "I know some people who write or lecture or just want letters typed. Perhaps I can get you enough work to tide you over, until things are better."

So he made a few telephone calls and went personally to see other prospects and Olive rented a typewriter and worked, when work was forthcoming, at her aunt's. She had her little car; she could call for and deliver the finished product.

Mary Karlin came home, and shortly thereafter her parents took her to the institution, and returned. Kim Sylvester returned, too, and Jonathan encountered him in the village. His lean face was brown and his eyes very blue against the tan.

"Hi-ho," said Kim, "the good and faithful physician. . . . I understand that Fran is no longer in the village."

"She's on a cruise."

"So I hear. I ran into mutual friends. Everyone's cruising — her parents are, I was, she is — quite a declension, isn't it? . . . Have you had an interesting winter?"

"Much as usual," said Jonathan shortly.

"You're not very expansive. Oh, well," said Kim, "I'll settle down in my attic — I've brought back some pretty fair sketches — and paint. And unless she changes her mind, Fran will be back."

Sophie had had several cards from her, Jonathan one. This cruise was somewhat longer than her friends had originally planned. She wrote to Jonathan, "Fun and games and a tiresome sun. I'd rather be back in Seascape."

Before she returned a sudden change took place in the Condit household. Sophie went to California.

She had always kept up with her classmates and friends, those from her high school, from Lister Memorial. She prided herself upon a large active correspondence. At Christmas the Condit box was flooded with mail. Many of the cards which came to Sophie had long messages on or letters in them. One was from a classmate of whom she had been reasonably fond, and who wrote that because of her husband's business they had moved to the West Coast. Eloise said she had made friends, but it was still a little strange to her. She was longing to see someone from the East. Did Sophie know if any of the people they knew were coming out? Did she ever come west?

Sophie had answered that card almost immediately, saying that she was considering a trip. "I've been rather boxed in here for a long time," she wrote, "and if Jonathan can spare me, I might – might, mind you – consider a trip."

Eloise had replied enthusiastically. Sophie must come, must stay with her; she'd have a wonderful time; the house was big and the children away, one married, two in college. . . .

So the letters flew back and forth and Sophie consulted a travel agency. After which, she said to Jonathan, "Do you think you could get along without me for a while?"

He said, "Of course."

Maybe she was going to the city for a weekend; or longer. She hadn't been since he didn't know when.

She said, "Well, good, though not flattering."

"You planning to go to town? I'd like to go with you," he told her, "but I can't, not at this time of year."

She said, "Jonathan, I'm tired. I haven't been anywhere except to town, now and then, since we moved here. I need a change. And Eloise Mathews has asked me to visit her in California."

"California?" He felt a premonitory pang.

She said, "I thought I'd fly out and stay a few weeks. No sense going so far and coming right back."

"Of course not."

"Mrs. Parker will look after the housekeeping." She regarded him doubtfully and added, "But there's the office."

Jonathan said, "I think I could get temporary help."

"Put it on that basis," said Sophie. She

thought so, too. Retired nurses and secretaries in Seascape were a dime a dozen. Then she said, "All right. If you can manage, I'll write Eloise and make my plans. I might stay a month," she said. "I don't know."

He felt as helpless as people often told him they were. He could not say, "Look up all the friends there, except Henry Stiles." The most he could do would have to be behind her straight back; he would write Henry. . . .

But could he say, "Look Henry, Sophie is going to California. She may just drop in on you?"

Chapter Eleven

Sophie, making her own plans, was also concerned with her brother's welfare. She had several names on a neat list; she could, before she left, interview possible candidates for him.

Jonathan said, at a breakfast, "Thanks, Sophie, but I already have someone in mind. In fact, I've asked her to take over during your absence."

Sophie was startled, curious, and affronted. She inquired, "For heavens sake, who?"

"Olive Evans."

Sophie was markedly aghast. She said, "You can't mean that!"

"Why not?"

"But – with all the talk . . ." Sophie began.

Jonathan Condit had a square and stubborn jaw. He said, "I'm not interested in talk. Susan Jarvis is a friend of mine and occasionally a patient. Her husband was my friend and patient. Olive is Susan's niece."

"Isn't it grandniece?"

"No. Anyway the degree of relationship doesn't matter. Olive is intelligent. She can answer a telephone. She can type and can get out bills, if any. Also, she needs a job."

"I think you're out of your mind! I won't have it," said Sophie. "That girl — she'll be alone here with you —"

Jonathan said, with dangerous and frigid calm, "This is my office, Sophie, and I'll hire whom I please. I am not given to rape. I am not contemplating asking Olive to sleep with me. Is that clear? I'm just offering her a job."

"Well . . ." said Sophie, and retired from the fray and the breakfast table.

In her room, distressed, insulted, and help-less, she even considered canceling her trip, then decided that she wouldn't — not even for Jonathan.

Arrangements had been easily made with Olive. She was to come in the morning, have lunch (if she wished) at the house, a victim of Mrs. Parker's ministrations; officiate on the telephone when Jonathan was absent and go home before dinner. He could manage the evening office hours. He'd already asked Mrs. Parker if, during his sister's absence, she would be willing to move into the small back-room suite and take the evening calls when he had to be out.

As for Olive's typing, she could use his machine or bring her own and work on that during the hours she was alone with nothing to interrupt her but the telephone. This arrangement would be flexible in terms of time, a month, more or less; but during that period there would be the little extra money and also, her typing work might pick up and therefore, when Sophie returned, she'd have more to occupy her.

Sophie, in the days remaining, was glacial. When she did speak, it was on household matters. Mrs. Parker, when instructed, said merely, "I know what I'm supposed to do," and when Sophie ventured to lay before Jonathan a long set of rules, warnings, and supplications he said mildly but firmly, "I'd be very grateful, Sophie, if you just went off on your holiday with a free mind and didn't try to run my life by remote control."

So his sister departed, torn between frustration, curiosity, and disapproval. Mrs. Parker moved quietly into a room with adjoining bath and equipped with a good radio and given the run of the study where the television was installed. Olive came and went at her appointed hours and used Jonathan's typewriter, thereby saving a month's rent, more or less, and life went on.

On the first day of her employment, Kim Sylvester turned up. He smiled, asked, "Do I know you?" and she said she thought not.

"Susan Jarvis' niece, aren't you?" He smiled again. He got around. He thought her oddly interesting in a plain sort of way, but Seascape's diagnosis, at second or third hand, enhanced her plainness. You never knew, thought Kim, about these small, seemingly insignificant women.

He told her his name, and she said, "I don't believe you have an appointment."

"Oh, no," he agreed, "but Doctor Condit and I are old acquaintances. I'll wait."

He waited in the reception room. Olive, rattling the keys and endeavoring to decipher an almost illegible manuscript — one created by a schoolteacher, who had a compulsion to write of her childhood in Maine — was somewhat distracted. She'd seen Mr. Sylvester about the village. She knew he was an artist. She also knew, seeing him at closer quarters, that he was an attractive man.

The waiting room filled up. Jonathan arrived, the procession began. And when Olive, coming into the office said, "There's a Mr. Sylvester — he hasn't an appointment . . ." Jonathan asked, one eyebrow lifted, "Is it an emergency? Or does it seem to you, Olive, that he has symptoms of leprosy or hydrophobia or whatever?"

Olive said helplessly, "He looks all right, Doctor."

"Then let him wait," said Jonathan.

When the patients with appointments had departed, Jonathan saw Kim Sylvester.

"Well?" he asked. "Or rather, how well?"

"I have a pain in my shoulder," said Kim. "Hurts like hell."

Jonathan said, "Take off your shirt."

He prodded a little and Kim made rude remarks. Eventually, with a slight inner satisfaction, Jonathan said, "Bursitis," that being an extremely miserable infection. "Not so bad, however." He produced a hypodermic syringe; he wrote a prescription, and gave some advice.

Kim said, "So thanks . . . That's a charming girl in the outer office."

"She's filling in for my sister who is away," said Jonathan imperturbedly, "although she's had no experience."

"Ah, so? as the Japanese are wont to say," murmured Kim.

"She is efficient," said Jonathan, and went on without a flicker, "If you derive no relief, come back in, say, a week, but in less time if the shoulder gets worse. But make an appointment."

Kim went away, and presently wrote to

183

Frances. He knew at which ports he could reach her, having obtained an itinerary from the steamship line.

"Darling," he wrote, "if you are really interested in your good and rather dull physician, you'd better come home. The formidable Sophie has taken off for California and there's a rather charming girl in the doctor's office, by name Olive Evans.... Pro tem, of course. How pro, I wouldn't know. Nor for that matter, how tem. Anyway, she appears to be the center of a small Seascape scandal, and has resigned from her school job. Personally I would not look twice at anyone whose job was, I believe they call it 'Home ec' but at this particular girl, three times."

It would be worth another dose of bursitis, which he genuinely had, to see Frances Lawson's face as she read that bit of information. Meantime, thought Kim, he'd find out a little more; not that Mrs. Simons, his landlady, wasn't a wonderful source of material. Researching Mrs. Simons' mind was like reading eight tabloids plus the headstones in the Seascape cemetery and all the resources of the Historical Society.

Frances received Kim's letter at the proper port and flew back from the next one. Waiting for her plane, after ignoring the plaints of her friends, acquaintances and cruise director, she cabled the woman who looked after the guest-house, who informed the Driftwood caretaker, who in turn informed everyone else. Frances reentered her own small domain after a fairly perilous drive which included ice, blowing snow, and a high wind.

Once established, she telephoned Mrs. James at her home and said she was ready to return to work, and then took herself to Jonathan's office. He was not there, but the waiting room was presided over by a small, gray-eyed girl, with obedient brown hair and a pleasant smile, who was busy doing something or other on a type-writer.

"Hi," said Frances, taking the measurements of the foe. . . . They were, she decided, pretty good, although not as good as her own. She then stated her name and said, smiling, "You're Miss Evans, aren't you?"

Olive acknowledged the fact and regarded Frances with extreme interest. Things get around. She then remarked, "I don't believe you have an appointment."

"No," said Frances, "and I'm not sick — except of traveling. I just came in to leave a note for Doctor Condit."

She left it and departed. It said: "Hi, Jon! I'm back in Seascape. How do you like them apples? . . . Frances."

Then she started for Little Driftwood, stopping off for dinner at the Inn.

She was sitting there, regarding black water and a snowy sky when Kim strolled in and sat down at her table. "I've had dinner, such as it was, but you could buy me a drink," he remarked.

"With reluctance," said Frances, beckoning her waitress. "What is your pleasure?"

He told her.

Frances said, "News gets around fast . . . sea grape vine, jungle drums furiously beaten from a convenient dune . . ."

"Oh," said Kim negligently, "I knew you'd rise to the bait. I've missed you. Have a nice cruise — as far as it went?"

"Splendid," said Frances. "And don't tell me how you've spent your time. I couldn't care less."

Kim's drink arrived, dry as the Sahara. He raised his glass and said, "To us."

"Thanks . . . *por nada*," said Frances.

"Darling Fran," said Mr. Sylvester, "you're being extraordinarily foolish — even for you. I'm worthless, of course, but talented and attractive. I love you quite a lot for a man of my execrable character. I also love your money. And we could have fun. We have the same tastes in a

186

number of things. You'd better marry me. I doubt you've had a more alluring offer."

"Several; two on the cruise, for instance."

"They didn't mean it," said Kim, "charming as you are. That's black magic — islands in the sun, moonlight on the water, deck games, and swimming pool. Doesn't mean a thing."

"One," said Frances, "was tall, blond, beautiful, divorced, and loaded."

Kim said, "If you're waiting for Condit, he isn't going to materialize. He's not your type, pet."

"Suppose you permit me to be a judge of that."

"Then, let's say, you're not his type. The little number in the office more closely matches the swatch, I think."

"Oh?"

"Wait till you see her!"

"I have," said Frances. "She's very pleasant."

"A man could do worse than marry a pleasant woman. . . . And I'm certain she's a good cook and housekeeper. Sophie picked the wrong time to go to California."

Frances asked for her check as the interested waitress hovered, and called the hostess — not Jenny, she'd gone to Florida — to say that she'd enjoyed her dinner and was glad to be back. Then she rose. She said, "Find your way home,

Kim. I'm tired. I'm going right to bed."

"I could make a suggestion."

"Don't."

He said, "Look, it's a lousy night. You wouldn't have to go far out of your way to drive me to my attic."

"Sorry," said Frances. "I'll send out a St. Bernard."

He followed her into the very cold night and to the parking space. "I could," he reminded her, "force my way into this little car."

"You could," said Frances, "and I could also chuck the keys in the water and go to the Inn for the night."

"How is your dear father?"

"I daresay, all right."

"And Maida?" He added thoughtfully, "What a mother-in-law she'll make."

Frances started the car. She said, "Every man for himself," and backed out.

The parking space was slippery. Kim, rearing back, slid and fell. It did his shoulder no good whatsoever.

He made a few choice remarks and went back to the Inn to buy himself another drink. He hated paying for his own drinks. It seemed so unnecessary. But sooner or later someone he knew would turn up and give him a lift.

Seeing Frances again, he realized that he was,

truly, as much in love with her as he could be with anyone. He knew she knew it. She was not deluded by the surface. He was as serious about her as he could be about anyone or anything, except his painting. As far as Maida Lawson was concerned, that was bilge water − and under the bridge, to mix a metaphor or something. She was not the first woman to toss herself at him; and she wasn't deeply involved; with Maida, it was only vanity, promoted by what he recognized as unhappiness. If it hadn't been for Frances, he might have amused himself more than he had. This had been at the root of their argument the night Mrs. Lawson had come down with the twenty-four-hour virus.

"Hi," he called, and waved at a couple he knew who were just being seated. He rose, his glass in his hand. "Mind if I join you?" he asked. "I've been stood up." He added mentally: Also knocked down, damn it. His shoulder really hurt. But that offered one consolation. He could go back to his doctor and see what was cooking in the reception room.

Jonathan telephoned the guest cottage that night. He said, "From your last postcard, I didn't expect you back so soon, Frances."

She said, "I was bored, so I flew back from sunshine, palms and commercialized charm. . . . How are you, Jon?"

"Fine — and you?"

"I'll live. How's Sophie?"

"She's written once, telephoned once; she's all right, I gather, and having a perfectly fascinating reunion with an old classmate."

"That's a nice girl in your office."

"I'm glad you approve."

"I didn't say that."

"How are your parents?" he asked hastily.

"Oh, they cable now and then. About now they should be buying out Hong Kong; at least, Mother, that is. . . . Jon?"

"Yes?"

"When's your next free evening?"

He told her and she suggested, "Dinner, here? I'll bake a cake."

He said, "Frances, I'm not sure — that is —"

"Don't try to get out of it. I know you're madly popular," she told him, "wildly social and all that jazz. But I've been away for a spell. Break your eighty-nine non-existent engagements, and bring Baffin to see me. Unless, of course, you're scared."

"Me, scared?"

"Yes, you."

He asked, "How's your ankle?"

"Pretty as ever," said Frances sweetly. "In fact, good as new, or, as they say in the TV ads, 'maybe even better. . . .' I'll expect you, then, by seven."

She hung up and went to bed, turned on the electric blanket and lay there, warm, comfortable, at home, but a little uneasy. She murmured, falling asleep, "So what if I have my work cut out for me, doubled in spades?"

Chapter Twelve

Sophie's friend Eloise Mathews lived with her reliable good-provider husband and their children – when at home – in a pleasant suburb of a California city. Eloise had put on weight since Sophie had seen her last and now wrapped herself in an expensive smugness as with mink. Sophie's room and bath – with a view ... an extensive vista of gardens and swimming pool – left nothing to be desired; and Eloise's hired hands, a haughty but exemplary couple, managed everything, including breakfast in bed.

Sophie, once having exhausted the news of mutual friends, found herself caught up in the whirlpool of furious activity which characterizes any suburb; sightseeing, luncheons, contract, movies, the Little Theatre.

Having ascertained before she left Seascape, that the town in which Henry Stiles and his daughter were staying was not far distant, she had, for courtesy's sake, let a week elapse before announcing to her hostess that she was going to

192

visit friends from Seascape who were staying nearby. Then she rented a car with which to drive the distance between Henry and herself, geographically speaking. Her first thought had been to telephone, but there was no listing, of course, under his name. So she had written a card and informed him that she might be passing through his town on the following Tuesday.

The card was inexplicably delayed. (Excellent as is the service of the United States Post Office, now and then a card or letter turns up dated, say, from World War One, or even the War between the States.) Hence, Henry had no warning.

Alice had gone to the Home. This was a normal procedure. Any man who appears in a strange town with a teen-age daughter who cannot adhere to the time-honored fiction of young widow — acceptable during any war — finds himself in a difficult situation when the teenage daughter exhibits certain overt symptoms. Hence, Alice went to the Home.

Henry wrote vague letters to interested parishioners, remained in the pleasant apartment, visited his child at least once a day, and embarked on a reading course. He had always wanted to read Proust but had never got to it until now.

For the rest, he took long walks, went occasionally to a movie, took short bus trips, and was incredibly lonely, as well as confused. His only grasp upon realism was his daily contact with Alice — whom he had come to know somewhat better than he had — and his letters to and from Jonathan Condit. All the rest was a nightmare in pretty surroundings.

He had, with misgivings, traveled Swann's Way, had penetrated Within a Budding Grove and, despairing of comprehension, was now embarked upon the Guermantes Way when Sophie's rented car drove up. He heard it, but did not even glance out of the window of his ground-floor apartment. When his bell rang in a determined sort of way, he opened the door and looked, staggered, at one of his most devoted parishioners. For a wild moment he did not know her because she was out of context; so might a man, trudging through the desert, encounter his own mother (whom he believes safely housed in Newport, Rhode Island) without recognition for a split second.

"Why . . . Sophie," he said.

Sophie said, "Henry. You're looking marvelous." And so he was for the California sun is potent . . . and then, added, "Surely you had my card?"

He answered feebly that no, he had not heard

from her in some time.

She explained rapidly that she was visiting in a nearby suburb and had just popped in to say hello.

She had timed it well: after luncheon, so he would not feel under any obligation to feed her; prior to the sherry or cocktail hour, and therefore well before dinner.

She said, "What a charming place!" and Henry, pulling himself together, said, "Oh, yes . . . we like it," and then, "Won't you come in?"

He took her into the living room which opened onto a sunporch, beyond which was a private patio, and relieved her of a handbag, a cardigan. She was hatless and her heavy fair hair was becomingly dressed.

"Where's Alice?" she inquired.

He said briefly that Alice was out.

"What a pity," Sophie said. "I did so want to see her. . . . Is she well enough to go to school here, Henry?"

Henry replied truthfully that he had been tutoring her, but that now there were outside teachers.

"You'll want to hear the Seascape news," said Sophie inexorably.

He did not. But he listened. There was nothing else to do.

At the end of an hour Alice had not returned

from her mythical errand or engagement and conversation flagged. Henry had not asked, "Couldn't you stay overnight with us?" – though she had come prepared for exactly this invitation, with a small but adequate flight bag in the rented car. He had not even said, "Do stay for dinner."

So she left. She left with him a card on which she had written her address and the Mathews telephone number. She said, "I'd so like to see you again, Henry. I – we have all missed you. And I do want to see Alice. I'm sure Jonathan would like a first-hand report of her progress."

Henry saw her to her car. He was confused, uncertain, and also angry. Returning to Proust, he condemned himself for his irritation. Sophie Condit was a good friend. She had every right to try to see him when in the vicinity. Although he had prayed without ceasing that his more affluent parishioners would this season prefer the Caribbean, Europe, or Florida to California, he had experienced for one insane moment, a compulsion to confide in his caller. There was no help she could give him, or advice, but simply to talk, to unburden himself, as he had only to Jonathan, might have eased his tension.

All Henry's life he had been protected by his parents, his chosen profession, and his belief in himself and in a benevolent higher power. He had also been guarded by his wife for as long as she had lived, and after her death, by his pastoral flock. Now he was no longer running the small, taut ship of his parish, no longer steering its spiritual course.

Sophie, driving back to Eloise's, remembered that she had said, "Don't wait dinner for me, I may not be back, in which case I'll phone." She was so distressed she found it difficult to keep her orderly mind on finding the right entrances and exits. She thought: What is the matter with him? He looks well, but he's aged. And if Alice is not well, why isn't she home and in bed?

Sophie hated mysteries. She never read those fictional puzzles which are contained between hard or soft covers. Forgetting that all life is mysterious, she despised the mysteries inherent in daily life – even in food. "What's in this?" she would demand if bidden to dine in some exotic restaurant where the lights were dim and the ingredients of the dish set before her unknown.

Whatever the mystery here, it had made Henry Stiles an unhappy man.

His smooth, gentle, rather over-worldly personality was still apparent – after all he'd assumed it almost as soon as he'd learned to walk – but beneath it, she was aware of his confusion.

Also, she was humiliated. He'd not wanted her there, and had been the reverse of glad when he saw her. She had seen the shock in his eyes, the fleeting expression – could it possibly have been fear? – which had crossed his face before he rearranged his features into a semblance of normal welcome. Why? Certainly it was quite natural that an old friend and a parishioner, finding herself in the neighborhood, would look him up.

She returned to the Mathews in plenty of time – neither their dinner nor plans were ruined – reporting that she'd had a pleasant visit with her rector and felt, while she spoke, a painful clutch in her heart which was not physical, nor was it entirely humiliation and affronted vanity; it was eighty per cent a deep concern.

He had not said that he might come to call on her, but had carefully explained that he had no car. He had not asked her to return, although he knew that for some little time she would be with her friends.

Sophie wrote to her brother. She said that, "passing by," she'd had an opportunity to see Henry Stiles. She added carefully, "When I dropped in, Alice wasn't there. I stayed perhaps an hour. They have a very attractive apartment. But there is something definitely wrong. I can't put my finger on it, but it worries me." She then asked how he was getting on and if Olive Evans was satisfactory.

Good Lord, thought Jonathan, dropping the letter as if it had burned his fingers. Later he wrote his sister. He said everything in Seascape was fine. He added that Frances had returned and yes, thanks, Olive was working out nicely. He said he was glad she'd seen Henry and he was sure that she had no cause for alarm, for as far as he knew, Henry Stiles was in excellent health.

Dining with Frances in the relaxed intimacy of Little Driftwood, Jonathan listened to her account of the cruise, his mind elsewhere. He was beginning to be a little alarmed at the manner in which Olive had taken over. She was, he conceded, grateful, as was her aunt; but she had begun to assume something of a proprietary air. Mrs. Parker didn't care for this development and said so. She also added, much to his astonishment, that she'd be glad when Sophie returned. Jonathan was aware that Mrs. Parker was not fond of his sister, that only respect was accorded. He had not stopped to figure out that the devil with whom you are familiar is easier to cope with than a horned stranger.

There were naturally times during the day when Olive and Jonathan were alone; and he found himself listening to confidences. The Karlin situation had not bettered since Mary's removal to the institution. Emily Karlin had taken herself off to stay near her daughter, where she had obtained work. Sam had moved into a rented room. His house was for lease on a month-to-month basis.

The rumor reached Jonathan that Olive was seeing Sam Karlin again, and he had spoken to her about it. He said casually, "I understand you're seeing Sam Karlin."

She said, her eyes wide, "I ran into him a couple of times — we had coffee together. . . . In a town like this," she added bitterly, "you can't even have a casual cup of coffee without people making a big thing of it."

"You're not being fair to your aunt," said Jonathan, "or, for that matter, to yourself."

She said, "Aunt Susan's found her own life. Oh, she misses Uncle Pete, she always will, but she's gone on. She doesn't really need me. I don't have much of a life. I didn't at home, I don't here. And the whole thing was such a misunderstanding. I mean about the Karlins — a misinterpretation. *That* wasn't fair. But, now that they're separated —"

"Who says so?"

"He does."

Jonathan sighed. He said, "I doubt if it is a terminal arrangement, Olive. When Mary's better — maybe even if she isn't — Emily Karlin will return." He reflected on the reports he'd had about Mary. One week progress appeared to be made; the next, perhaps, she'd have to be put under restraint.

"She shouldn't have gone if she cared about him at all," said Olive angrily. "He's having such a bad time — all the worry and the debts."

He said gently, "Except as a friend, that is not your concern."

To his horror she began to cry. He brought her a glass of water and spoke to her quietly, wondering uneasily if Mrs. Parker was within earshot or if a patient might turn up. Olive said, when the short outburst was over, "I'm so lonely. . . ."

"But your aunt said that you had made friends —"

"They dropped off after my resignation." She added, "There's been nothing wrong, Doctor, between me and Sam Karlin. He — he just likes to talk to me."

Sam had said that, too.

Now, at Little Driftwood, his hostess complained, "You haven't heard a word I've uttered

– deathless prose, too."

Jonathan conceded that he hadn't been listening carefully.

"O.K.," said Frances cheerfully. "Is there anything you can keep your mind on? Scrabble, a cross-word puzzle, a game of double solitaire, or do I have to go out and break a leg in a deliberate bid for your attention?"

He laughed. "I'm not very good company, Frances," he said.

"No. Although," she added thoughtfully, "I prefer yours, even when bad, to anyone's. I suppose it's the doctor image to which we have been exposed in the last few years."

"Image?"

"Certainly. . . . Casey, Kildare, Hennesy – and that marvelous gentleman in *Gunsmoke*, to say nothing of the psychiatrists, the hospital heads and the various minor boys in white drifting about the screen."

"I haven't time to acquaint myself with their goings-on."

"You should take a course," said Frances. She rose and snapped a finger at Baffin, who opened one eye and then shut it again. He liked her very much, but she couldn't give him orders, certainly not when Jonathan was present.

"Baffin," said Frances, "take the man home."

She went to the door with them, smiling; and Jonathan said, "Forgive me. I'm working on a couple of puzzles of my own."

"That figures," said Frances. "See you around. Happy solutions."

He drove home, half his mind preoccupied with Sophie, three thousand miles away; the other half with Olive.

Happy solutions!

These were not among the answers in the back of his book. As far as Sophie was concerned his hands were tied. He had warned Olive and also, earlier, Sam Karlin. There was nothing more he could do.

It was, he reflected, reactionary that the old plodding G.P. was expected to be father confessor, psychologist, marriage counselor and a shoulder to cry on. Specialists in their various fields had few such problems; there were trained medical psychologists as well as psychiatrists. The majority of patients rode the efficient assembly line. . . .

"Dobbin, the stumbling dray horse," said Jonathan to himself.

Never become emotionally involved with your patient. That was an axiom. Listen with sympathy, and then send them to priest or minister, job counselor, guidance center. You're supposed to deal with their medical problems.

But if they didn't end there?

Oh, hell, he thought, driving into his own yard and noting that Mrs. Parker had left the lights on in welcome. I'm tired, I guess.

Mrs. Parker had not left a note for him on the hall table, so he judged that no one had called. She was upstairs looking at television. He could hear the barking of a fast-drawn gun. Mrs. Parker's personal life was devoid of drama nowadays. She liked violence if, in the end, the good man won.

Baffin went leaping upstairs. He was very fond of television.

Jonathan prepared to follow him; he'd look in on Mrs. Parker and then go to bed, resigned to the fact that, if she planned to watch all her favorite programs, the guns might speak far into the night.

As he turned off the outside lights, he heard a car drive up, and opened the door. The stars were frosty in a dark sky and Kim Sylvester was carefully decanting himself from a small car.

He came up, his overcoat slung around his shoulders. He said, "Sorry, I should have phoned. But my shoulder is giving me unadulterated Gehenna, so I borrowed a car and set off — impulsively, as usual."

"Come in," said Jonathan, leading the way to the office. "When did it get worse?"

"The night Fran came back. We had a slight discussion in the parking lot of the Inn. She drove off in a tantrum, I skidded on a hunk of ice and fell."

"Why haven't you come before?"

"I did consider it that night. But instead, I went back to the Inn and resorted to the orginal pain killer, Whisky. . . . Or was it gin? I've forgotten. Then it seemed to let up, and I had work to finish — a commission. But today I couldn't even paint, damn it!"

"Take off your jacket and shirt," said Jonathan, with a sense of history repeating itself. He had to help his patient.

A moment later Kim yelled and then remarked, "Low level of pain, that's me. Low level, period."

Presently Jonathan said, "A hard wrench, nothing more, but the inflammation is considerably augmented. I'm going to give you a shot. It helped the last time, I think."

But Kim was muttering, "Serve her right if I sued her!"

"She didn't run over you," said the doctor callously.

"How can you be so unfeeling? I remember the painting — often reproduced on calenders — of the lamplit room, the adorable little patient, and the physician beside the bed, fingering his beard, and looking concerned. . . ."

"I remember it, too."

"Probably sat there all night," said Kim, sighing. "Hey, that hurts! I've told you I'd like to paint your portrait. It may be the only way you'll be paid for professional services unless I can finish this commission to the satisfaction of the highly neurotic and extremely rich old bag who thinks she wants it. Anyway ... let's talk about your portrait, hypo in one hand, shillelagh in the other, and an expression of infinite calm. Might add a stethoscope around your neck. . . ."

"What would you call it?"

"I think, 'The Lonely Man. . . .' Give me a hand here, will you."

Jonathan gently poured his patient into shirt and jacket and Kim suggested, "As a final gesture, drape my topcoat about me. The Barrymore touch, or perhaps Orson Welles. No, I'll settle for Bat Masterson, without the cane."

Jonathan went out to the car with him. He asked, "Can you drive without too much discomfort? If not, leave the car here, I'll take you home."

"*Gracias*, but my friend requires his car for early-morning transportation – he does an honest day's work," said Kim. "I'll get back all right. Stiff upper lip, covered with the sweat of pain. Bite on the bullet. Thanks again."

"If the shot doesn't help, come in tomorrow and we'll try something else."

"Arsenic?" asked Kim, and put the car in gear.

Jonathan went back to the house. He had not liked Kim Sylvester, one hundred per cent; now he disliked him only ninety-eight; for the remaining two per cent, he liked and was sorry for him. Sylvester, thought Jonathan, was disquietingly discerning.

Jonathan's special kind of loneliness had nothing to do with his environment. Nor was it caused by lack of friends. It was not based on the fact that one winter day a young woman had slipped on brownstone steps and struck her head and died. That had been a different kind of loneliness. That it had lessened was natural . . . time, the healer. That wonderful cliché, which was also a truism. How often had he promised a patient's wife, husband, children, this miracle. Too often, he thought. His particular loneliness was rooted in the effort to reconcile a split personality, to become integral; to cease to be ambivalent. In him there was the man who stands apart and is objective; and the man who draws close and is subjective. It was also due to the basic awareness that knowledge *per se* was not enough — the knowledge which came from books, from studying, from listening, and then gradually, increasingly, from experience — medical knowledge. Once you went past that and permitted yourself to become involved in matters beyond the minds and bodies of your patients, you were hooked, and, God, you were lonely.

You could have a hundred friends, a dozen siblings; you could have parents, a wife and children, and you'd still — within yourself, because of your temperament and your profession — be inexplicably alone.

Chapter Thirteen

A few days before Sophie Condit was to leave for the East, she had a telephone call. She scarcely recognized the voice which spoke to her . . . the voice which asked, in a curious half stammer, "Sophie . . . ?"

"Yes," Sophie said, and Henry Stiles went on, "Could you possibly come. . . . I mean, as soon as you can?"

She thought: Alice . . . Alice must be worse, possibly critically ill. She said, in her strong, confident voice, "I'll be there as fast as a car can take me, Henry."

She told Eloise, round-eyed with curiosity, only that Dr. Stiles had called and asked her to come; she added, throwing things into the flight bag, "His daughter – she's one of Jonathan's patients – must be worse. And he doesn't know anyone well here, Eloise."

She called the rental agency, a car was sent around, and she told Eloise, "I'll be back as soon as I can. I think perhaps I'd better cancel my flight. . . . The ticket's in my brown case. Would you do it for me, Eloise? I don't know how long I'll be needed. Once I know, I'll arrange another flight – that is, if I'm not putting you out. I can always go to a motel."

Eloise said, of course, it wouldn't be putting her out. Sophie must come and go as she pleased.

She said that night to her husband, "There's more in this than meets the eye."

"Think that up all by yourself? Nice woman, your classmate. But it's pleasant to be alone with you, honey."

Eloise said thoughtfully, "I bet you a dollar she came out here just to see whatever his name is."

"Well," said her husband, "she'd make a good wife for a clergyman. Run the parish without half trying. I'm so glad I married you, darling, you can't run anything, which is, of course, why you run me!"

Sophie managed to get to the Stiles apartment house without being arrested. She left the flight bag in the car. To prepare is one thing but to anticipate, another. She hurried up the path and rang Henry's bell. He opened the door at once, a completely distraught man. He said, "You came –"

"Of course," she said soothingly. She walked past him into the living room.

He said incoherently, "I thought when you came here first, it was because you'd heard something; because you were curious. I — I disliked you for it. God forgive me."

"I just came to see you," said Sophie, "and Alice." She added, "There is something dreadfully wrong, isn't there, Henry? Is it Alice?"

After a moment he said, "Yes." He added, "If I don't talk to someone, I think I'll go insane."

"You can talk to me," she said.

"I thought you knew . . . or guessed," he said, "or that Jonathan had said something."

"Jonathan doesn't violate his patients' confidence even to me," said Sophie.

He said helplessly, "It's being so alone here . . . not knowing what to do except to wait, and not knowing what to do after that, really. Then when they called me, just before I telephoned you —"

"Who called you?" she asked, "and about what?"

So he told her, stammering, with pauses between the sentences, but as badly as was possible.

"She's gone into labor," he said, "prematurely. They didn't want me there yet . . . they said, it would disturb her to see me. I was to wait until

I was sent for . . . the telephone hasn't rung."

Sophie was rigid with shock, but her mind functioned. She said, "I'll be here, Henry. I'll go with you, if you like." Then practically, for it was past two o'clock, she asked, "Have you had lunch?"

"No . . . Sophie – I –"

"I haven't either. Where is the kitchen?"

He showed her and she opened a refrigerator door, glanced into a supply closet, and into cupboards. "Go back into the living room, Henry. I'll make tea and sandwiches," she said.

She watched him shamble out and set about boiling water, measuring tea leaves, slicing bread, opening a tin of chicken, and looking for lettuce, butter, mayonaise and condiments. There was a bottle of sherry in one cupboard, and one of brandy. She chose the brandy, poured a stiff measure, added the ice and water, and took it to him. She said, "Drink this – I'll be back in a moment."

She returned a few minutes later with the tea and the sandwiches. "Try to eat something. You can't help Alice by starving yourself. . . . Now begin at the beginning," she said.

He did so, feeling the burden lighten. He was probably insane to tell her anything at all. But for a great part of his life he'd permitted people to talk to him, to release their tensions through words, casting their burdens on someone who was equipped to listen, to be objective, sympathetic and to counsel. Now it was he who talked, as he had with Jonathan.

Sophie said after a while, "Alice is young and strong. She'll come through this all right; and when she's well you can take her home. You have the proper — excuse. Jonathan sent her out here with you because she —"

"Required a change of climate?" he interrupted. "Yes, of course. But I keep thinking about the baby."

"If it's normal and healthy," said Sophie, "it will be adopted. . . . There's no other way, Henry."

"I know," he said miserably, "but I'll be haunted for the rest of my life . . . My grandchild, Alice's child —"

"Henry," said Sophie, "Alice is only sixteen."

"I know."

He managed the tea and one sandwich. Sophie ate all her sandwiches and had two cups of tea.

The telephone rang, Henry rose and went toward it. His hands shook as he picked it up. She heard him say, "Yes." She heard him say, "I'll be right there."

When he turned away, he was paper-white and there was a blue line about his mouth.

He said, almost inaudibly,

"She's all right, but the baby is dead."

Sophie thought: Thank God. Aloud she said, "I'll drive you over, Henry, and wait for you outside. There's no reason for Alice to know that I was here."

She spent that night in Alice's bedroom in the apartment. She cooked dinner for Henry Stiles. He was half dazed from the ordeal of waiting, and of seeing his daughter, her young features drawn, lying quietly in the hospital bed, with the tears running down her face. "I know," she kept saying, "I know I would never have seen him, but to have him die . . . Do you suppose," she had asked her father, "it's my fault because I wasn't supposed to have a baby? Is that why he died?"

Henry had seen the tiny premature infant. He had made the heartbreaking necessary arrangements. Alice might one day grow up, marry, have children, but there would always be − for her father if not for her − this small, uncomplaining ghost.

Most of the night at the Stiles apartment Sophie sat up, and talked to Henry Stiles. He asked her half a dozen times, "Was it my fault?" He asked, "How can I make it up to her?" He asked, "What are we to do now?" He said, "The baby wasn't baptized."

214

She answered each question.

She did not think it his fault as much as the fault of the times. She said, "There's no way to make it up to her, Henry; you'll just have to help her as best you can." She answered, "You will wait until she is strong enough to travel maybe a little longer than that, and bring her home ... and you must, if you can, persuade her to finish school and go on to college. As for the baby's baptism," she said gently, "I am sure God understands."

At the moment Henry Stiles was no more sure of God than of himself. He took Sophie's hand and held it in a hurting but impersonal grasp as if he were drowning and she a stranger.

By dawn she knew more about Henry Stiles, his marriage and his personal difficulties, than he himself knew.

She said eventually, "Try to sleep now. You can go back to the hospital after you've slept. I think you should write to Gavin as soon as you are able."

He said, "Sophie —"

"Henry," she said, "If you are afraid that I will say anything ..."

"Oh, no," he said, distressed and humiliated, "but —"

"I know. The parish and the Guild; and the talk, the gossip, the wanting to know. . . . I've been through that for four or more years. Have you forgotten," she asked, "that I am a nurse . . . and I know that confidences are privileged? I'll not only not mention this to anyone, I won't even speak of it to you —"

"Jonathan," he began.

"You're his patient, and so is Alice. He must be told that I was here."

He said humbly, "Please tell him."

"All right." She rose. The dawn was golden, and in its light Henry Stiles looked old and bleak and haggard. She said, "I'll take you to the Home — and then I'll go back to Eloise's. I'll fly home as I planned to. Perhaps I can still get the flight I canceled. If you need me before then — call me."

At noon she fixed eggs and coffee and toast, packed her little bag, drove him to the hospital entrance of the Home and said good-by. She touched his hand briefly. She said, "I know it will be difficult, but bring her home when you can. Not yet awhile. Perhaps in the spring. And I'll talk to Jonathan when I reach home."

"I can't thank you —" he began.

She said, "Don't try," and drove away.

She was not shocked in the usual sense of the word; she had seen too much. She had been stunned at first. Now she was herself again. She would keep her promise. She would not presume upon his confidence. Alice would never know that Sophie Condit had spent a long night with Alice's father, and listened to him talk, had seen him weep, and heard him pray. . . .

He had trusted her; the trust might waver; in fact it was almost bound to do so. But he would see that he had not misplaced his trust. He had needed her these last hours. He would, perhaps, need her again. She had not felt as happy, as confident, and as useful since before Jonathan Condit married his young wife, Edna.

Arriving at Eloise's, she said briefly, "It was nothing very serious after all. His daughter was ill – the doctor thought a possible appendix – so Henry took her to the hospital for tests. It was an appendix, all right; I stayed during the surgery. She's just fine, no complications . . . Jonathan will have the report, of course, and I can make a first-hand one to him. I'll call the airline, if I may, Eloise, and see if I can get the flight – you canceled it, didn't you? – that I'd intended . . . or possibly an earlier."

She managed an earlier one, and telephoned Henry, saying only, "How is she?" and then, "That's fine," and after that, "I'm going back sooner than I expected. I'll see you, come spring, in Seascape."

She flew out of the sunshine into the chilling

end-of-winter ice and snow and had never felt warmer in her life. Even the trip to Seascape — in another rented car, sliding about the roads — did not daunt her.

She left the car at the town nearest Seascape where it could be picked up, and taxied the rest of the way home. She had wired Jonathan the night before leaving, so he would expect her. When she reached the house, the lights were on and Olive Evans just leaving.

Sophie, allowing the taxi driver to cope with the luggage, said, "Well, how are you?" and Olive said she was all right, thank you, and escaped into her own little car and drove away.

"She's been crying," said Sophie to herself. "Now what?" But Olive and her problems could wait. She had something to tell her brother.

She told him after dinner.

"Henry called you?"

"Of course. You don't think I'd force myself on him?"

"Why, yes," he said mildly, "I do; that is, if you took a notion."

She said angrily, "The first time I saw him, I didn't know anything was wrong ... I still thought that it might be he who was ill and not Alice."

"He wasn't. Anyway, you went to see him, and you admit he wasn't happy to see you."

"Naturally he wasn't. . . . Now that I know the situation, I can appreciate that."

"But," said Jonathan thoughtfully, "you were near at hand; and when the going got rough, he turned to you."

She said, "Well, he didn't know anyone else —"

"Very fortuitous," said Jonathan. Then he smiled. He said, "I'm glad you were there, and glad you could help him, for you did, I'm sure. The next job is to see that he helps Alice. He's a good man, Sophie, but a weak one. I'm sure you've discovered that."

She had; but she said nothing, folding her lips severely. A man's weakness can be a woman's strength. A man in whole armor is wonderful, but formidable; find the chink the armor and you can break through and perhaps claim him for your own.

Jonathan said after a moment, "Well, have it your own way. You're a grown woman and he's supposed to be a grown man. But if you use your knowledge and, I'm sure, your sympathy as a sort of emotional blackmail —"

Sophie turned scarlet. She asked, shaking with anger, "What on earth do you mean?"

"My dear Sophie, you know quite well what I mean. You've had your sights trained on Henry Stiles for quite a while. But Henry has been quite happy as a widower; happier, I'm certain, than when he was a husband. These charming, highly spiritual men marry only because it's expected of them."

"Jonathan!"

"I am not impugning his original normal virility, Sophie," said her brother, "and remember it's said that it is better to marry than to burn."

She interrupted. "You haven't."

"Married, no; burned, yes; but if the flame was too hot I could quench it casually. Not Henry . . . and anyway, I daresay he hasn't burned in a long time." He looked at her with a sudden compassion which both humiliated and soothed her. He said, "Sophie, actually I'm glad this happened. You were there when you were needed. Whether or not he will continue to need you, I don't know, nor do you. Give it time; meanwhile, forget what happened."

"Forget?"

"Yes, to all outward appearances; it will work out, one way or another. And no one knows of this except you and me, Henry and Gavin, Alice herself, poor little devil, and the people at the Home. And they are, of course, uncommonly close-mouthed or they wouldn't be there."

She spilled some coffee and he said, "You're

tired. I'll give you a mild sedative and then you go to bed and sleep for twelve hours."

She rose and, in passing, put her hand on his shoulder. "But I haven't asked about you," she said.

"There's nothing to tell . . . the same old round only more so."

But she pulled herself together to deliver one swift arrow.

"Why," she inquired, "was Olive Evans crying when she left this house . . . just as I came in?"

When he did not answer, she went on to bed.

Chapter Fourteen

Sophie was home once more, so things would presumably return to normal. Mrs. Parker was pleased. Now she could go happily back to the small house in which she lived alone. Some people are like this; they prefer to return after the day's work to the dark, quiet cocoon they have spun for themselves. Baffin was pleased also. He was by no means ecstatic, but he'd bestowed a small unexcited kiss upon the back of Sophie's hand when she'd come in. Jonathan was neither glad nor sorry; she had, after dinner, given him too much to think about. The only person who grieved was Olive. Jonathan had explained, after Sophie's wire arrived. he had said, "I'd like you to finish out the week, Olive."

Well, that had been their arrangement. She could work in the office daytimes until his sister returned.

At breakfast, with Mrs. Parker in the kitchen, Sophie asked again, "Why was Olive Evans crying when I came in last night?"

He said, "She has certain difficulties."

"None of my business?"

"None whatever, Sophie. I can say, however, that she is also probably sorry to be leaving. She liked the work, for the short time she had it."

"What about her typing?"

"Oh, she's managed to get enough to do. Perhaps I can find another full-time job for her ... out of Seascape, in another town."

"I see." That's that, thought Sophie. I suppose she thought it she were here, day after day ...

"How's Frances?" she asked.

"She's fine."

"I must get around to see her," Sophie said.

"Olive's staying the week out; that will give you time to go calling, unpack, write your bread-and-butter letter."

Sophie said sharply, "Don't be silly. I can manage without Olive."

He was stupid, Jonathan thought, to feel guilty about Olive. But then everyone feels guilty half a hundred times in a lifetime, with or without reason.

Olive had wept on his shoulder after the last patient had gone yesterday afternoon, and Mrs. Parker was occupied in the kitchen. She didn't, she said, know what to do or where to go. She'd believed, by coming to her aunt she was doing Susan a kindness; and she herself had thought to make a place for herself here in Seascape, make friends. . . . His own mind had added silently, "and influence people." But everything had gone wrong. Unhappy as she'd been at home, she wished she'd never come here.

He had tried to quiet her; he'd said, "We'll find something for you, Olive" . . . and then added that she could finish out the week.

She did not. She telephoned at breakfast time and when Sophie answered and came to Jonathan, saying, "It's Olive Evans . . . she sounds a little − odd," he had said he'd take the call in the office.

"Olive?" he asked.

She answered in a small tight voice, that she wasn't feeling well.

"I'll drop by and see you as soon as I can."

"No," she said. "Thank you just the same. If you don't mind − if you can get along − I won't be back. It really isn't worth it," she added, "for just a few days."

Jonathan said he could manage; and told her to call him if she felt worse − or, ask her aunt to call.

He was scowling thoughtfully when he returned to the dining room and asked Sophie for

224

a hot cup of coffee. "That one's cold," he said childishly.

"How could it be? You weren't gone a minute." But she rang for Mrs. Parker and asked for a fresh cup and saucer, before saying, "What's the matter, Jonathan?"

"Olive isn't coming back," he said. "She says she doesn't feel well and it's not worth returning for the few days."

"My idea exactly," said Sophie briskly.

Jonathan went to the hospital, secure in the knowledge that Sophie could cope with telephones and patients. She would also look carefully over the house for evidence that Mrs. Parker had slackened (she had not), and she would scrutinize the office. She'd be quite happy, he thought. But he wasn't happy about her, or Henry Stiles.

To do Sophie justice, he had not said when she left for California, "Be sure you don't look up Henry." It could not, therefore be held against her that she had.

He went to the hospital; he came home for lunch and made a few house calls. On an impulse he made his last stop at Kim Sylvester's.

Mrs. Simons, a pleasant woman shaped like, and cheerful as a robin, greeted him happily. She said, "I do hope you've

225

come to see poor Kim."

"I have."

"I told him he should call you."

"He didn't," said Jonathan. "I'm psychic." Which reminded him of Frances, and he thought: Sometimes I wish I were, and sometimes I am and wish I weren't.

He climbed the stairs to Kim's enormous one-room-and-one-shower lodging. There was a kitchenette corner, a gatelegged table, a bed-couch, some chairs, and a great many paintings. The place smelled of turpentine, paint, whisky, and fried eggs.

He knocked.

"Stay out," said Kim.

Jonathan went in. He found his patient sitting gloomily in a large shabby chair, his arm in the sling Jonathan had recommended.

"What the hell are you doing here?" demanded Kim. "Go 'way. I can't afford even country St. Lukes."

"Social call," said Jonathan, and sat astride of a chair. "Mrs. Simons said she'd told you to call me."

"Down with women," said Kim, "always interfering."

"You're worse?"

"Hold it. I'm not. Actually, I'm better. This whole damned thing is psychosomatic," said

Kim, "except the fall on the ice; and that, on Frances' part, was probably a death wish — my death."

Jonathan said, "It's always interesting to listen to a lay psychiatrist. Why psychosomatic?"

"I hate it here," said Kim furiously. "I don't like myself. I can't paint."

"I'll contradict you if you wish."

"I don't give a damn what you think. I know how I want to paint. Also, there's Frances."

"Yes?"

"I've given up," said Kim. "So she's a part of the pain in my shoulder. And there's her mother."

Jonathan waited and presently Kim said, "I feel absurdly guilty about Maida. . . . I wasn't entirely truthful with you."

"I doubt you were," said Jonathan.

"Oh, you know so damned much," said Kim, "you make me sick. Well, O.K. I'm licked on all counts, so I'm going away."

"Where?"

"South. No yachts this time. I know a place and I won't tell you where it is. The fewer people who know about it, the better. Friend of mine has a sort of shack. It's adequate. I can have it. It will be cheaper than this attic. Also, no problem of getting free rides. You walk most places. Food's simple, the heating problem doesn't exist — or if it does, there's a pot-bellied stove. All a hurricane can do is blow you into the gulf. The sun's a healer, you know. Want to come with me?"

Jonathan, to his astonishment, found that in a way he did. He said just that. "In a way," he answered.

"Good. Well, don't. I'm lousy company, as you may have deduced. But I'll get well and I'll do some painting, and it won't be any better than it has been, but at least I won't keep on kidding myself that it could be. I might even start a Gifte Shoppe," said Kim. "Serve me damn well right. Meantime, I'll beachcomb. I'll be, as my friend says, a beachnik."

"Strange as it may seem," said Jonathan, "I wish you luck. What can I do for you now?"

"Pills I don't need, shots I don't need, so give me enough money to fly south, tourist. In return, when I'm back at the easel, I'll paint you the best damned picture I'll ever paint."

"How much do you need?" asked Jonathan.

Kim considered and then told him. He added, "That's enough to get started. I have enough to pay off La Simons, and I'll throw in the furniture. I'm going to leave the paintings at one of the galleries; they might even sell one or two. I'll have my gear shipped out."

Jonathan produced a folding check book. He

said, "I haven't the least idea why I'm doing this. But it's a deal!"

Kim said, "You're doing it because you don't want me on your conscience."

"How do you figure that out?" asked Jonathan. He handed the check to Kim.

"Oh, you feel you should do something about me; make a man of me perhaps; see that I cut down on the sauce. I do, I assure you, when no one's around to set up the second and third rounds. Reform me so I don't go chasing after pretty, rich, neurotic women, and their daughters. Remove me, too, as a threat to Frances."

"I doubt you were ever a threat," said Jonathan.

"You're probably right." His eyes blazed a brilliant blue as he looked up at Jonathan. "You ought to get away," he said. "Physician, heal thyself! Personally, I think you've had it. I don't know why, but there it is."

"Maybe you're right."

"Too many people," said Kim, "too many women, and an inability to make up your mind, except medically."

"That's a fair diagnosis," Jonathan agreed. He got off the chair and looked at Kim who said, turning the check over in his fingers, "wait a year and then write this off as a bad debt."

"When are you going?"

"As soon as I get this cashed and arrangements made. It won't take long."

Jonathan asked, "Any doctor near where you'll be?"

"Oh, thirty, forty miles. Why?"

"You may need one."

"I won't," said Kim. Then he brightened. "Come to think of it, my friend told me last time I saw him that the old doctor had died and that the new one was a woman; young and pretty enough." He grinned suddenly. He said, "She's the only doctor around that district. Maybe she could support me."

"In which case she would need psychiatric help."

"Oh, I don't know. I'd make someone as good a husband as the average," said Kim.

Jonathan said, "Well, happy landings."

"You don't think you'll ever get the painting, do you? Wait and see," Kim said.

Jonathan was laughing as he went downstairs and when Mrs. Simons bounced out of her own quarters to twitter anxiously, "How is he, Doctor?" he answered, "He's fine, just fine."

And he was, too, Jonathan thought. He'd probably prescribed his own cure; also, he'd done — and by himself — what most people tried to do with medical help. He'd admitted a fact or two and faced a couple of other facts

230

squarely, after his fashion.

On Sunday, Jonathan stopped at the Little Driftwood to have lunch with Frances. She had asked Sophie too, but she had refused. She had to finish her settling, she said. "You run along," she told Jonathan. "I'll relay any calls."

There were none for the short time he was in the guesthouse. And presently Frances said, "Kim Sylvester is shaking the Seascape sand off his feet."

"Yes, I know."

"You do? How come?"

"You didn't know he'd become a sort of peripatetic patient?"

"His shoulder? No, he didn't tell me."

"When did you see him?" asked Jonathan.

"Let me see. The night before Sophie came back, I think. He roared up here in some kid's hot rod, with the infant driving, shouted to him to come back in an hour, horsed in, and demanded a drink."

"He tell you about his plans then?"

"Oh, yes," said Frances. "Personally I think he's tired of it here. His beachniking or whatever he calls it won't last long, but —"

Jonathan asked, "Is he going to send you a painting in return for your check?"

231

"How did you —?" She stopped and stared at him, and then said, "Oh, no!"

Jonathan nodded, and then they both broke into helpless laughter.

He asked after a while, "Who else in town, I wonder?"

Frances counted on her small, spatulate fingers. "Oh, there must be half a dozen of us," she said, "who could manage his escape. . . . I'm going away, too, Jon."

"Again?"

"My parents are due home next month," she said. "I'd better be there when they return. But I'll be back."

By the time the winter had melted into early, reluctant spring, there was a small shift in the Seascape population. Frances had gone back to the city, Kim Sylvester was in the south — now and then he sent Jonathan an illegible postcard depicting unreal palm trees and coral sunsets — and Olive Evans had returned home.

Her aunt came to see Jonathan. "It didn't work out," she said.

"I'm sorry."

"I am, too. I thought she'd be company for me, but she wasn't, after all. You just can't fit in that easy; she couldn't, I couldn't."

"But what about her people?"

232

"Oh, they took her back all right, and the talk died down there long ago I guess. Only they'll make it hard for her. I don't know what she'll do either."

"She's a perfectly capable girl," said Jonathan, "and there are other jobs besides teaching."

"I know, but she was trained for that. Well, I just wanted to thank you for all you did for her."

"I did nothing," Jonathan said. "I tried, but that's not enough."

She looked at him through the eyes which were like her husband's except that hers had been washed clear by solitary silent tears. She said, "I guess that's all anyone can do — try."

It was at about this time that Jonathan began to dream of Edna again. He had not, in the first year following her death, ever dreamed of her. Sometimes, hopefully, he would sleep; but she did not come, with her young and vulnerable face loving and radiant.

After that, occasionally he dreamed. Usually they were walking together down an unfamiliar street or road; sometimes the road was scented with lilacs and sometimes flaming with autumn leaves, and usually he could see the ocean.

If they talked — and waking he never remembered — what was it they had said?

Now he dreamed again; he saw her clearly, but she was smaller than life, a little figure, far ahead on the road. And when he tried to catch up with her, he could not. His feet were clogged with earth.

But always in these recurrent dreams, she turned to him that young and radiant face, loving, compassionate, and understanding; and sometimes she spoke his name and he would wake and stir uneasily in his quiet room, and Baffin would pad over to stand beside Jonathan's bed and ask in his own way, "What's the matter?"

Nothing: except that Edna had receded, gone on, without him — very young and, to him, lost.

He began to wonder, going on his ordinary rounds, if something were seriously wrong. After three years, the dreams again, but they were different now. He no longer woke from them with the sense of guilt.

I'm tired, he thought.

It was quiet on the Seascape front. People had colds or a virus; one man, putting his lawn mower in shape, cut himself badly, a number of children came down with the ordinary diseases of childhood. And then there was the accident.

An eighteen-year-old boy, out of high school, not going on to college but, by having worked summers, buying himself an old car, which he drove furiously on the highways and the curving secondary or country roads.

Jonathan knew him. He had taken him through various minor crises for the past four years; he'd known his parents before he had come to Seascape to practice.

The boy – his name was Caleb – was badly hurt. The ambulance came, and the wrecking car. The parents came; and Jonathan, in his car, followed theirs to the hospital. The surgeon Jonathan most trusted had been called.

A cubbyhole was found where Caleb's parents could wait until Jonathan went into the operating room with the surgeon, the resident in surgery and the nurses. He came back to tell the parents everything that could have been done, had been.

He sat by Caleb's narrow bed and watched the eighteen years ebb away, despite everything and he thought: Why?

Later, Jonathan went home with Caleb's parents, leaving the empty hospital room to sit with them in their stiff little parlor. He had prescribed the usual sedatives. They would not take them.

"Maybe I wasn't hard enough on him," said Caleb's father heavily.

He was a big, dour man. Perhaps when Caleb was very young, his parents had maintained the discipline they themselves had known. But times changed.

"We argued," said Caleb's mother. She looked drowned. "We begged. But for the last two years . . ."

For the last two years Caleb had gone his own way; and because his parents had felt that he was now grown and that if they intervened he would dislike them, they had not intervened. There were certain rules which had been ignored.

"He was safer," said Caleb's mother, "when he was just a little boy and believed that although we denied him things he wanted, we were older and wiser . . . he was safer," she said again helplessly.

But for the last two years he had done as he pleased, coming home to meals, going to bed when it suited him, watching television until half the night had gone, going out on parties with people his parents had never known. . . .

"We did the best we could," said his father.

They had, according to their lights and the permissive philosophy of the era in which Caleb had grown up — to smash himself to pieces against a stone wall, and after a little while, to die, patched up, but not enough, in a hospital.

"Don't take it so hard," said Sophie when she

heard Jonathan come in at dawn, and came from her room to see him climbing the stairs, his face a curious mask of grief and resentment.

All he said was, "You're so sensible, Sophie. I envy you."

Chapter Fifteen

It is wonderful to be sensible. The Jungling boy was dying. He was thirteen. He'd had leukemia for several years. Transfusions, new drugs had kept him going; if you could call it that. Now he was really going. . . .

Jonathan was with him when, eventually, he went his — to Jonathan — uncharted, lonely way. His parents were there also. He was the oldest child and the only son.

Nice kid. When Jonathan first came to Seascape to practice, the Junglings had brought the boy to him; he'd broken his left wrist falling, playing tree tag. Sturdy, blond, intelligent, with a freckled candid face. . . .

A year later he'd come again, by himself; his mother had sent him around; they lived near the Condit house, so he walked. He had had some bruises on his arms; at first he hadn't paid much attention; kids are always getting bruised and not knowing when or how. But when the bruises appeared on his body, his mother was

238

worried. She'd say, "It just isn't natural."

It was natural enough; a great many mysteries in life are natural; and in death, also.

O.K., so he'd had three years or so. . . .

People always ask why . . . looking across a hospital bed, or waiting in an impersonal room, or walking up and down a little parlor at home. Why? . . . Why? . . . Why our boy?

Why anybody's boy? why Pete Jarvis? Why Edna? Why a hundred — a million — people? Why?

There is no physician on earth, no matter how much he knows, no matter how qualified to give the medical answers, who can answer that one to the questioner's satisfaction.

Sophie was sensible about it, as about everything. She said with validity, "You did all you could."

"It's never enough."

The shrouded enemy sits in a corner of a bedroom, or on a stone wall against which a car has been hurled, or in the hospital room or laboratory, and bides his time. So you fight him, sometimes, with success.

The Jungling boy died. But Frank Haber — senile, and cared for by a harassed, dutiful, loving daughter, who would not have him "put away" — was ninety-two and alive, thanks to antibiotics, to medical wonders, and geriatrics.

Why?

So after Caleb, the Jungling boy died, but Frank Haber kept his lease on what you could technically call life. So the population kept on shifting, ever so slightly, and when the spring broke, greening along the dark boughs, Henry Stiles and his daughter Alice came home, in time for him to take the Easter services.

Alice, slender and a little tanned, did not return to school; she would in the autumn. She was tutored for the rest of the spring term by a retired teacher; she saw her friends again. She had fully recovered, her father told his concerned parishioners.

Those who saw her thought she had somewhat changed; she was as withdrawn as ever, but she had, it seemed, somewhat matured. When questioned about California, she was apparently quite open. She'd liked it there, she said.

She came to see Jonathan, of her own accord. Her father brought her and waited, as she'd asked him to, in the car, until Sophie came out and said briskly that perhaps he could do with a cup of tea.

Sophie having retired from the waiting room to the living room, Alice folded her hands in her lap and said unnecessarily, "I'm back."

"Yes, I'm glad," said Jonathan. "How do you feel, Alice?"

It was a routine question, but what else could you ask?

"I'm all right." She lifted her young eyes to his. "And thank you – for everything." She added, "My father's been wonderful – and Gavin."

Jonathan said, "They love you, Alice."

"I know. Maybe," she went on, searching for words, "love isn't enough. I mean, I don't know what I'd have done without it, but you're so lonely."

He said gravely, "There are things you have to do alone, no matter how much others love you; one – in a sense – is to be born; another to die . . . and still another, if you're a woman, to have a child. No matter how much help you have, you must go through it alone. There's no turning back."

"It hurt," she said childishly, and then she said, "They didn't want me to see him. They did say it was a little boy."

"Yes, I know."

She said, "I suppose maybe sometime when I'm grown up I'll have other children, if I get married." Her eyes widened. "But I don't suppose I should ever get married. . . ."

"Why not?"

241

"I'd have to tell, wouldn't I, Doctor Condit? Wouldn't I?"

This was something he'd heard before, too. He said, "When the time comes, Alice, you'll have to make that decision."

"I never liked babies much," said Alice. "They scare me, the littlest ones. I was always afraid to hold them. I thought perhaps they'd break."

He knew what she could not articulate: Someday if I'm fortunate, I'll be married and secure; I'll have a baby, perhaps a son — but I'll always wonder what my first son looked like.

She said, "I was pretty sick. . . ."

He said, "Alice, you have your life ahead of you. You must do the best you can with it. No one can do more."

"I've kept up with my studies. I'll make it back to school, and I'll go on to college," she said.

"Do you know what you want to be?"

"No. Sometimes I think a nurse; sometimes I think I'd like to work in a lab. I don't know, really."

He said gently, "There's time."

Time. The wound would heal. The memory fade, and the scar tissue thicken.

In the living room Henry Stiles was saying painfully, "I don't know what I would have done without you, Sophie."

"Nonsense," said Sophie. "I just happened to be there."

"I wonder if anything really happpens . . . ? Well, there's not much I can do except thank you again," he said.

"You didn't tell Alice that I —"

"No, of course not."

"She'll be all right," Sophie said in her confident way. "She'll go on as if this had not occurred."

"You don't really think that, do you?"

"No. But why say anything else?"

He was slightly ill at ease, saying, "Sophie, if at first I thought you'd come to ferret out something, I apologize again."

"You were vulnerable," she said; "it was natural you'd think that, though it wasn't true."

"I know."

"We're all so glad you're back. The parish missed you."

"I've heard nothing but good reports of Joe Merrow," he said. "He's done a good job; carried on. No man is indispensable. Perhaps I thought I was. I worried a good deal while I was away. Pretty soon, I suppose, people will be coming to me again for help with various problems. I thought for a long time I could give it. Maybe I did. . . . The trouble was I believed that as a man made in God's image I'd been trained with His approval. I'm not so sure now."

"Oh," Sophie said, "you'll help a hundred times more than you ever did, just because you are vulnerable."

"I hope so," he said heavily. He added, "I've learned that two boys in the junior class have left school." He looked at her anxiously. "I couldn't help wondering —"

She said, "That gets you nowhere, Henry."

That evening she asked Jonathan, "How did you make out with Alice?"

He said, "She has considerable strength of character, Sophie. As she said, she'll make it, but I don't envy her the struggle."

"Her father has his struggle, too."

"Of course. He can no longer see himself as omnipotent."

"You're not being fair. It was a dreadful thing for him to go through."

"It wasn't exactly easy for Alice," he said evenly.

"I'll never understand that girl —"

"She doesn't ask or expect anyone to understand her. Her problem is to understand herself."

Sophie said doubtfully, "I wonder what the people in the parish think."

"That's not your concern. Most of them don't think much at any time; at least not beyond the

244

narrow circle. There are always rumors in any — shall we say — closed corporation? Some founded; other, not. Alice will have to accept the lifted mental eyebrow, the unspoken question, the delicate prying. So will her father."

"Aren't you a little hard?"

He did not answer.

Impersonal, just pity is one thing; it is not an emotion; it is a state of mind rather than of heart; a rationalization, a proper distribution of understanding, once you have ascertained the facts. Personal compassion is something else again. You can't see the picture in toto; never as a whole, just in bits and pieces. Pick up this piece; look at it; pick up another. They are sharp because they represent shattered images, shards, broken patterns of living — and because they are sharp, you cut yourself. So you are angry — not with the people who have caused you to experience compassion, but with yourself.

Jonathan remembered a good many people who, when those they loved became ill — slightly, seriously, even terminally — were angry, too; not with the doctors or the nurses, but with the patients. These were the people who thought: How dare he — or she — do this to me, cause me this anxiety, this suffering? But the base of their anger was fear.

245

Frances Lawson returned to the city in time to meet her parents' ship. It was after midnight a week or so later that she telephoned Jonathan.

The bell rang, Baffin barked, and Jonathan, switching on a light, reached out a long, naked arm and picked up the instrument. His mind, which had been clouded with sleep and beset with dreams, was, from long practice, instantly alert. He answered mechanically, "Doctor Condit speaking."

"Jon, it's Frances. Everything's in the most dreadful mess possible."

"What do you mean?"

"I can't tell you over the telephone. I'm not calling from the house either. I have to see you, Jon."

"You'll drive up?"

"I can't. Is there any way you could come here, perhaps stay overnight at a motel? I could have dinner with you."

He said, "I can't tomorrow, Frances. But the next day." To his astonishment, she was crying. She'd said she never cried. "I can get in by dinnertime. You don't want me to come to the house?"

"No, please, not to the house."

He told her the name of the motel where he usually stayed when he was in her city, and asked if she would make a reservation for him.

246

After the conversation was over, he lay smoking for a little while. One should never smoke in bed. . . . But he was wide awake. He propped himself up against the pillows.

Sophie knocked at the door, and came in to ask, "You have to go out tonight? I heard the telephone."

"Frances called," he said. "There appears to be some family trouble. . . . I've said I'd drive down day after tomorrow and spend the night. I'll be back next morning. I can get Banning to cover for me for that short time."

"Did she tell you what was wrong?"

"No, Sophie, she didn't. Do go to bed."

"You shouldn't be smoking," she warned him.

He put out the cigarette and said, "Run along like a good girl."

Dr. Banning was agreeable despite the distance to be covered between his bailiwick and Jonathan's; and at the hospital, Jonathan had, at the moment, no critically ill patient on his list.

He drove to the city in which Frances lived and checked in at the immaculate, unspectacular motel.

He thought she looked wretched, her face was drawn, her eyes shadowed; she also looked less elegant than usual: good tweeds thrown on, her lipstick blurred, her fair hair hastily combed.

He left her in the lobby and was conducted to his unit. He needed a shave, he thought; yet had shaved that morning.

When he rejoined her, they went into the dining room and he asked, "Could you do with a drink?"

"A light one."

The restaurant was only half filled and they had a quiet corner table.

"It's your mother, isn't it?" he asked when they had ordered.

"Yes. . . . There was an ambulance at the pier; the ship's doctor arranged it. My father wouldn't let her be taken to a New York hospital. I went in the ambulance and McKenzie followed with father in the car."

"What happened exactly?"

She said, "It's hard to find out; he's so absolutely furious. But — she tried it again; two days from port."

"She'd been drinking?"

"Not during the entire trip. Yet she had no help, none at all. Can you see what that must have done to her?"

"Yes, clearly."

"All she got out of it was sobriety," said Frances, miserably. "I suppose that was enough for him. Sobriety, so he needn't worry when she went to the lunch or dinner table, or played contract at night. Sobriety and nerves that were raw and —"

"Don't try to describe it, I understand."

"If she goes off again," said Frances, "drinks, I mean — and her doctors here think it's very likely — that will be the end, one way or another. Or maybe she'll hit on the right dosage or method before that."

"What have they decided, Frances?"

"She's going to a sanitarium," Frances said. "She'll have the works, a suite, round-the-clock nurses, the best psychiatrists. They'll watch her. They say they can cure her. Perhaps . . . but I don't know how you heal a person's soul."

"I don't either," said Jonathan.

She said after a moment, "My father insists that I remain at home with him."

"Why?"

"He manufactures quite a full social life — it's in layers. He does considerable entertaining at one or the other of his clubs at lunch, or when he goes to New York, Chicago, the West Coast. But he likes to entertain at home, too. Entertain is rather a misnomer. Often that's business too, the men he sees at the clubs, but with their wives, once the wives are screened," said Frances. "Then there's the purely un-business end of it; this is the layer he married, let's say; and relatives. He is concerned with relatives unto the fourth or fifth generation. . . . A few of his have been successful ... Mother's were born in the top drawer. Anyway, some he bullies, and some he defers to, and to those who are a little hard up, he sends checks and baskets of wine on holidays."

Jonathan said, "He doesn't have much fun, does he?"

"None that I know of – or, if by fun you mean extra-marital indulgences –"

"I didn't, as it happens."

"Well, there've been some, however discreetly organized." She looked at him with despair, "I can't say I blame him. No, I don't at all, considering the situation."

"You haven't said why he wants you to stay with him."

"I thought I had. He needs a hostess ... while Mother is having what must be conveniently called her breakdown due to exhaustion."

"Has it occurred to you he is lonely?"

"Of course he is. He's always been, I suppose, since he was a little boy, living in a respectable dingy sort of poverty. I imagine when he was grown and making money – tons of it, eventually – that compensated for a time. I assume when he married he thought he'd never be lonely again."

"He married for love?"

She said, restlessly pushing aside her almost untouched plate, "How do I know? My mother was beautiful, in her way; she was also a rung on the ladder money couldn't buy for him – or so he thought."

"What are you going to do?" Jonathan asked.

She said, "I came to ask you."

"You'll have to decide that yourself, Frances."

"I knew you'd say that. I don't want to stay here. I want to be at Little Driftwood. I like it there. I have something I've never had before – privacy, a certain amount of – peace, I suppose you'd call it. I like the people I know, or most of them; and the work at the hospital. And that, you'll say, is being selfish."

"No."

"My father says it's my duty to stay with him. He mentioned that I'd been a grave disappointment; 'the breakup of my excellent marriage' – those were his exact words – my refusal to fit in with the paternal pattern, 'always rushing off somewhere,' he said. He did not say that he needed me, except, of course, as a hostess and a sort of proper shoulder to lean on."

"Will you be permitted to see your mother?"

"Not right away; after a while. He's not to see her at all, I believe, at least for a considerable length of time."

"Compromise," said Jonathan.

"Compromise?"

"Life's mostly that," he said smiling, "and the thought isn't original with me. Why don't you come back to Seascape, return to town occasionally when your father has some special festivity planned and when you're allowed to see your mother?"

"Mind if I ask you something?"

"No," he answered, conscious of uneasiness.

"Do you want me to return? . . . Incidentally, Driftwood won't be opened this summer or if it is, just weekends, if father takes a fancy to come up."

He said, "Yes, I want you to return, Frances. But because you want to, not because I want you to."

She said, "All right. I'll be back in perhaps a week. I wish you'd tell Mrs. James that when you go to the hospital tomorrow. What time will you be leaving here?"

He said, "In time to get home for breakfast, after fortifying myself with coffee en route. I have a job to do."

When they were finished, he took her out to her car. She said, walking across the parking lot, "I'd like to stay here with you tonight."

After a moment he said honestly, "And I'd like you to, but you're not going to."

"No." She stopped by the car and looked at

him under the bright glare of the parking lot lights. She said, "When I was in your house for those few days, I left my door open a couple of times at night."

"I saw it."

"And the times you were at Little Driftwood —"

He said, "The telephone always rang, fortunately."

Frances laughed. "I'm no one's wife," she reminded him, "not even Potiphar's."

"I'm aware of it."

"You are difficult to seduce," she said thoughtfully. "Perhaps on neutral grounds — not my house, not yours, and not, of course, a city motel?"

Jonathan laughed. "It is written that men prefer to do their own seducing."

"Oh," she said, "that's what they think. Good night, and thank you," she added. "See you around."

Jonathan went back to the motel, left a call for five-thirty, and went to bed. He'd bought an evening paper and a couple of paperback novels in the lobby. He tossed them aside within half an hour and lay there thinking. He was, he knew by now, in love with Frances Lawson. It had not been as a sudden blaze of light, a ringing of bells; it had come by degrees and was complicated by emotions of pity, of tenderness, and the desire to understand her. His recognition of it had been arrived at with impatience, even annoyance.

To fall in love was one thing; to love, another. And he had no taste for remarriage. It wasn't a question of remaining faithful to a memory — technically he'd not been, these years since Edna's death. But marriage implied personal responsibilities, and also a sharing of himself, and this was something he did not wish to do again. It had been easy to share with Edna because . . . Why? he thought. Because she had been younger than himself, and immature. Because sharing with Edna had been simple; she'd been a listener, a sounding board? Who could say whether or not this would have altered had she remained with him for the rest of their lives?

He sighed, turned out the light, and spoke to Baffin before he remembered that Baffin was not with him, that he was alone in the impersonal motel bedroom.

Chapter Sixteen

Sophie's natural curiosity, Jonathan thought, driving home through a cold and misty morning, would scurry in all directions like ants scattering from their anthill. But, when he walked into the house in time to sit with her at breakfast, he was agreeably surprised that she asked no more than had he had a good trip? And how was Frances? She added that he looked tired.

He answered that the trip had been all right, Frances was well and would return presently to Little Driftwood, and yes, he was tired.

Perhaps she listened, perhaps not; she seemed unusually preoccupied. But just before he left the house she imparted one piece of information: it was rumored, she said, that Sam Karlin had sold, or was in the process of selling, his share of the store to his partner.

He wondered briefly why Sam hadn't stopped in to tell him; which was, of course, absurd. The sale of a business interest is a business matter. Sam had never been Jonathan's regular patient, nor had his wife; Mary had been Jonathan's patient and Doctor Marod sent him, from time to time, reports on her condition, which were not encouraging.

That afternoon Jonathan, leaving the hospital, stopped to see Mrs. James in her office and deliver Frances' message, and Mrs. James said, "I'll be glad when she returns; we've all missed her."

On the steps of the building he ran into Roger Banning, whom he liked very much. He had covered for him a number of times and could rely on Banning to do the same for him. Banning was an excellent medical man, older than Jonathan by something over a decade. He had been born in the village where his office now was. Jonathan had been associated with him a number of times professionally, on consultations. He admired and envied the older man's attitude. His patients were tenaciously loyal to him, although as Jonathan recalled, during the several times when he had taken over the practice, two or three had complained fretfully that, as Dr. Banning grew older, "it seems like he doesn't take a personal interest."

Observing him Jonathan sometimes thought: "The mixture as before." For Roger Banning's manner toward his patients was briskly sympathetic if sympathy were indicated, understanding, and quite detached — dispassionate if you prefer.

They walked toward their cars in the thin sunlight, and Banning said, his brown eyes narrowed, "You're looking lousy, Jon."

Jonathan said, "Well, thanks. I went away for the evening and night, came back early this morning. Long drive."

"I hope it was for pleasure."

"Not exactly."

"Pity," murmured Banning. "How long since you've had a checkup?"

"Oh, a couple of years, I think."

"Two and a half to be exact. I have total recall. Make an appointment, neglect your patients for an hour or so and come see me."

"There's nothing wrong with me," said Jonathan, half amused, half irritated, "except I'm tired."

"A common complaint, and usually a symptom, whether it's physical or emotional fatigue," said Banning and got into his car. He was a prosperous and relaxed man. He had a delightful house, an equally delightful wife and a couple of children. And was probably, Jonathan thought, the sort of physician who, leaving the office, would not take his patients home with him, but would leave them locked securely

257

and safely in his files.

As Jonathan drove home, it occurred to him, with a slight sense of shock, that he'd been tired for a long time; and that, since he was not yet forty, he should more quickly recover from the end-of-the-day fatigue.

Perhaps Banning was right; a checkup was indicated.

A week or so later, he made the appointment, going straight from the hospital to Banning's office. Banning's nurse, whom he knew, said pleasant things, including the fact that he would not be kept waiting long. He wasn't.

Sitting beside Banning's desk he replied to questions he himself asked almost every day of his life. Yes, he was often tired; yes, there were times when he did not sleep well.

There were questions which weren't necessary in his case; such as: How much exercise do you get? A good deal, if it came to that, in and out of a car, up and down stairs.

Banning said, "You don't have much fun, to you?"

Jonathan considered that and then answered smiling. "If you mean golf, skiing, hunting, dancing, getting drunk — no."

"Ever take a break?"

"You know when and for how long, Roger."

"When you first came to Seascape to practice," said Banning, "if I recall correctly, you had a boat; you even went fishing."

Jonathan said, "There doesn't seem to be much time."

"Then you'll have to make it." He regarded his patient and confrère with wise, quiet brown eyes. He said, "I learned. But then I had to if I intended to see my wife and children."

Jonathan had heard that one before from a number of physicians and surgeons; somehow they managed a compromise.

"Well, let's take a look at you," Banning said.

Later he said, "Your blood pressure's up considerably." He looked at Jonathan's chart lying on his desk; there was very little on it.

Jonathan shrugged. He asked, "Whose isn't?"

"You're in pretty good shape," said Banning, "but you do need a rest."

"That's what I tell my patients. Most of them can't afford it."

"I'm not suggesting that you go to Europe," said Banning sharply. "Merely that you take a couple of weeks off and go away somewhere and try to relax. I don't know how you prefer to relax . . . if it's in a city under the bright lights, O.K. If you'd like to crawl off somewhere, be entirely by yourself and not see anyone but the milkman, that's fine, too. The method is up to you. Write your own prescription. But if it's the isolated life, I've a cabin not too far away – trees, a fireplace, the usual conveniences if not the luxuries – and you're welcome to it. Think it over."

"But –"

"Oh, hell," said Banning, "it isn't summer yet; and the worst of the winter practice is over. Get yourself in shape for summer, Jon. The blood pressure will probably come down, with rest. I'm reasonably certain it's not organic. But if you keep on driving yourself –"

"I work no harder than anyone else," said Jonathan. "How's *your* pressure?"

"I could join the Marines tomorrow," said Banning, "as far as that's concerned. I don't think it's work that shoots yours up. I think it's you."

"Maybe I should see Marod?" Jonathan said, and grinned.

"Psychogenic, sure; psychopathic, no," said Banning. "Go away, get some sleep, get out of doors, have a stiff drink before dinner, chop some wood, read some books, take naps, and while you're doing it, manage a good long look at yourself."

"I may just take you up," said Jonathan, and thought with sudden longing of fresh spring days, and deep quiet, of cold nights and silence; and solitude.

"You'd better," said Banning. "Otherwise, you'll be dress rehearsing for a coronary."

"The doctors' dilemma," said Jonathan.

"Exactly."

He rose and they shook hands. And Banning said, "Call me, if you decide on the mountains — change of environment, that's good you know. There's no telephone in the cabin. There's a neighbor down the road, name of Hank Johnsen. He has a phone and you can leave the number with your sister in case anything world-shaking occurs. Other than that, no one can reach you; you'll have a time finding the place, yourself." He struck Jonathan on the shoulder, a sharp short rap. "Go home," he said, "and ponder. I can get around to see your patients in or out of the hospital, and I won't keep you posted unless something happens and I have to." He fished in the desk drawer, produced an envelope, and a marked map. He said, "I lend the place now and then. Everything essential is here; even a list of what's to be had in the village which is six or seven miles from the cabin. And Johnsen's name and all that. The key's also in the envelope. The cabin will be in shape. Hank caretakes. If you decide to go, call me, and I'll notify him."

Jonathan weighed the envelope in his hand.

It appeared to contain quite a big key. He asked, "What's it going to cost me, Roger?"

"Professional courtesy," said Banning. "Then while resting Chez Banning, your food, drink, gasoline. But what it will cost you if you don't follow my advice, I don't know yet. Perhaps I won't know for a year or two, but eventually I'd find out and so would you. And then whatever it cost could be plenty."

Jonathan went home. He said nothing to Sophie. She would ask questions, call Roger Banning, flap around generally. Besides, he wasn't going away. Why should he? What's a little rise in blood pressure? He encountered it every day in other people. Up on Wednesday, down by Friday.

Frances wrote to him. She said, "Don't look for me for another week or so. I've written Mrs. James. Everything's in an uproar here. Between being furious with me, my mother, and probably himself, my father is boiling. You've never been to New Zealand, have you, and seen the boiling mud? Well, he's like that. Bubbles all over the place. His doctor is giving him tranquilizers. . . . I'll have to stick around for a while longer. Meantime the only person who has ever been able to get along with him, his sister Charlotte, has announced she's coming for a visit. This will rearrange things. He's always looked after her financially and she thinks he's on God's doorstep. She'll console and soothe and be enchanted to manage menus and guests, if any."

Before the week was up, Jonathan had a telephone call from Susan Jarvis. She said she was all right but if he had time, could he stop by and see her.

He made the time at the end of an afternoon's rounds, and found her brown and fragile as an autumn leaf.

"What's the matter?" he asked, sitting down in Pete's old chair.

She said, "Olive . . ."

Olive, he knew, was back with her parents. He asked, "They've been making it rough for her?"

"I don't think so . . . or — well," said Susan, "nothing she wasn't accustomed to — but she's gone. I had a letter from her mother."

"Gone? Where?"

"They don't know. She just left, bag and baggage, in her car. She said she was going away on a trip and and they'd hear from her, later." She paused; and then she said, "I don't know that this has anything to do with it, but you heard Sam Karlin sold out?"

"Yes."

"Well, he's gone, too," said Susan. "A few days

ago. Gave up his room, stopped by the post office, said when he had a forwarding address he'd let them know, and pulled out."

Jonathan said, "But she wouldn't be so . . . Oh, come, it's a coincidence."

"I wish I thought so."

Jonathan said thoughtfully, "But what would they live on?"

"Sam's not old, and he's strong enough; he can always get some kind of work. Olive, too."

"Mrs. Karlin would never divorce him," said Jonathan. "If what you think is true, Olive must be out of her mind."

Susan said, "Daresay. I just thought I'd like to tell you. I haven't said anything to anyone else and don't intend to." She looked at him with old, unhappy eyes. "I'm sorry for her." Then she smiled, a little. She said, "I sort of hoped that after you got to seeing something of her you might — well, like her. She thought a lot of you."

Jonathan did not pretend to misunderstand. He said, "I'm afraid that's one prescription I couldn't write. But why take off with a man like Sam Karlin? Olive's young and attractive. Good Lord, there must be a half dozen suitable and eligible men around."

"Oh, there were," said Susan. "But seems as if she doesn't want to get married, not really."

"What makes you think that?"

"Because she never had a steady beau," said Susan. "Lots of opportunities, but none steady. Seems as if by her own choice. And that man at home, and Sam here, both married. Seems like that's what attracted her — them being married."

"Could be," said Jonathan. "Let me know if you hear anything, will you?"

She said she would and went to the door with him. "Thanks," she said, "for coming. I used to talk over things with Pete."

Jonathan could hear Pete expressing his opinion. He knew just what he'd say. "Damned fool girl," and then, "poor kid."

He went home and at supper Sophie said she hoped he wouldn't be called out that night because she had an engagement. There was a social meeting of the Guild. The color rose a little in her face and she added, "Well, not exactly a meeting. Henry called and asked if I could come over and talk to him."

"Run along," said Jonathan. Sophie had assumed the presidency of her small group, and she was in and out of the parish house nowadays whenever it did not conflict with what she considered her duty toward her brother.

There were few patients that evening and Jonathan went upstairs early and, for Banning's sake, watched a Western and then went to bed. He was conscious of tension, and of being tired again – not again really, simply more tired than usual. He thought: I'm susceptible to suggestion. Damn Banning anyway.

But it was absurd at his time of life to stand at the foot of a short flight of stairs and wonder if he could drag himself up them. It didn't make sense. Nor did it make sense to fall suddenly and heavily asleep over a page in a book which could not hold his interest, and wake up an hour later, with no sleep in him, at least not until it was almost time to get up again.

This had been happening on and off. Now and then he took a mild sleeping pill, but it was a habit he did not want to acquire. Usually he woke from the burden of the unrestful sleep and the fragmentary dreams and lay there, willing his long body to be quiet, or turned on the light and tried to read again.

He tried to explain matters to Baffin, taking him for an early morning run on the beach, saying, "I ought to do this more often"; or "How you can get into that ice cold water beats me." He went on, to Baffin, "So I'm half dead nights and feel sluggish in the morning and come to, maybe midafternoon, for a while. If someone came to me and told me this about himself, and after examination, I found there

266

wasn't anything organically wrong, as good old Roger would say, I'd ask, 'Do you like your job?' But when I ask myself, the answer comes up, 'Yes.' It's the getting wound up in it I don't like. I've been fighting it for a long time now, wondering if the day will ever come when I can be an observer, a spectator. I don't have to get into the fight; all I'm supposed to do is referee it."

Baffin shaking himself, and walking sedately beside his idol, remarked that there must be something he could do about it. As a matter of fact, said Baffin, we could go away somewhere, just the two of us.

It was about a year since Pete Jarvis had died. It had not seemed a particularly significant year, during the living of it — but now it did. Jonathan thought, going back into the house, of a number of things and people . . . of Frances and Olive, of a boy named Caleb, of the Jungling boy . . . of Maida Lawson . . . of Sam Karlin. He also thought of Kim Sylvester and at breakfast, he said to Sophie, "I wonder what's happened to Kim Sylvester."

"Oh," said Sophie. "I knew there was something I meant to tell you, but I've been so busy lately." She appeared to fall into a small reverie and started when Jonathan said, "I'm listening."

"You remember the Owens, don't you? Summer people. I think you've had them here at the office, the children anyway."

Jonathan concentrated a moment and remembered.

"They're up here," said Sophie, "or rather Mrs. Owens is. They're putting an addition on the house. I ran into her in the post office a day or so ago. They're just back from Florida, and they saw Kim Sylvester there."

"Beachcombing?"

"Painting," said Sophie; "and taken up by some rich widow or divorcée or whatever. She's going to back a show for him there, and maybe next autumn in New York. Mrs. Owens said he looked very well, tanned of course, and he'd put on weight."

"Who's the unfortunate woman?" Jonathan inquired.

"If she told me the name, I've forgotten. But Mrs. Owens said she was hanging on to his arm and looking up at him as if he were Rembrandt."

"Well, good for Kim," said Jonathan. Bully for Kim, who could solve his own problems. He thought: Maybe the rich whoever she is isn't unfortunate after all. Maybe all Kim needed was an adoring woman with a million bucks who'd think he was Rembrandt. It might compensate for his knowing he was not.

He remembered fleetingly that Kim had spoken of a woman doctor, in the area of his beach shack. She wouldn't have done at all, thought Jonathan; she wouldn't have time to hold his hand or the money to back a one-man show. No hen medics for Sylvester.

He rose, said, "I've a phone call to make," went into his office, shut the door, and called Roger Banning.

Chapter Seventeen

He did not tell Sophie his plans until that evening, and then he did so abruptly.

"I'm tired," he said, "and I haven't had a holiday in a long time. So I'm taking off early Friday for about two weeks."

She asked, stunned, "But — where? I just couldn't, at such short notice. . . ."

"I'm going alone," he told her, "except for Baffin, and as to where, Roger Banning offered me the use of his mountain cabin and I've accepted."

"Doctor Banning?" She looked at him and inquired sharply. "You've been to see him as a patient?"

"That's right. Sophie, get that look off your face!"

"What look?"

"Two, really. One: You pop right into bed and I'll take care of you. Two: How can you be so inconsiderate when I've so much to do?"

"Nonsense," said Sophie. "Just the same,

you might have told me."

"There's so little to tell. I met Roger by chance at the hospital a while ago. He suggested I have a checkup; I hadn't had one in some time. Eventually I went to see him. There's nothing wrong except being tired. So his advice was that I go off somewhere and give myself a break before the tourist season sets in. To that prescription he added the offer of his cabin. I believe he hunts there autumns, or goes there when he can get away for fishing."

"I'll call Doctor Banning," she said, "and talk to him *myself.*"

He said quietly, "You'll do nothing of the kind." Not that Banning couldn't cope with her, he thought. "I am, strange as it may seem to you, a grown man and a doctor. Roger is also adult and a physician. And to anticipate any questions, I'm not departing in order to crack up or to crawl into the woods and die. I'm going away to be by myself and to rest. And you are not to interfere."

She said, "I didn't mean to be interfering, Jonathan. But how am I to reach you?"

He put his demitasse cup on the coffee table and reached into a pocket. He said, "Here's the address and the rural route number; also the telephone number of Roger's neighbor, Hank Johnsen — in case of a valid emergency, but not

271

otherwise. Roger will cover for me, Sophie, and everything will be taken care of. Just refer all calls to him."

She said meekly that she would. She did not dare to question him further. Once in a hundred years Jonathan told her not to interfere. She had not forgotten how she had tried, for his own good of course, when she learned he and Edna were to be married. On such rare occasions her brother reminded her a little of their father, of whom Sophie had always been slightly afraid.

She wondered: Has he quarreled with Frances? But no, he wasn't sufficiently interested in her to quarrel with her. She thought: Could this have anything to do with the Evans girl? I wonder where she lives now? Olive, who had left Seascape rather suddenly and whom, prior to that, Sophie had seen weeping as she left the Condit doorstep.

I must ask someone's advice, she thought. So she contrived to see Henry Stiles, and tell him how worried she was, and on Thursday evening Henry drove over to see Jonathan.

"This is nice," said Jonathan. "I didn't expect you. I hope nothing's wrong."

"Oh, no, indeed. I just came on impulse to — er . . ."

"Anyone I know?"

Henry looked uneasy. He said, "Well, frankly, I saw Sophie and she's alarmed about you."

"She has no cause," Jonathan said. "I'm all right. Roger Banning will tell you so if you ask him. I'm not planning anything desperate or spectacular such as murder or suicide. I'm simply going away for two weeks. Why should it be so difficult? Honestly, Henry, I haven't had two weeks off since I was an intern, except for an occasional leave in service." He thought: Haven't I? Didn't Edna and I have two weeks together once?

"I believe you," Henry said. "But you know how women are."

"We both know."

"Anyway, perhaps I can reassure Sophie," said Henry, and Jonathan added that they might be able to do it as a team, and since the last patient had gone, surely Henry could be persuaded to come into the living room where Sophie was, and have a glass of sherry?

"Wait a minute," Henry said. "I'd planned to come see you soon anyway, and when Sophie said you were going away, I felt it must be tonight."

Jonathan waited.

Henry said, "She's been wonderful. I can't tell you how much she has helped me." He looked anxiously at Sophie's brother. "Alice likes her, and so does Gavin. I haven't asked her to marry me, yet" — he seemed visibly to brace himself — "because I wanted to talk to you first. I know she has you to consider."

Jonathan said, "Sophie gave up a good deal when she came here to be with me — I'll always be grateful to her. By now I think she knows that I'll be able to manage without her. After all, she wouldn't be far away, and nothing would make me happier than to see her married to you."

Henry said nervously, "Thank you, Jonathan.... I don't of course know how she feels."

Which was odd, because Henry had always thought he knew how Sophie — and other women — felt about him. But even that minor type of self-confidence had recently been shaken.

Jonathan thought: This is a big step for Henry. Bigger than the one he took when he had married young. And so far he'd been successful in evading the second time around.

But he was growing older, was Henry. He had also sustained a hard blow, and the shock of it was still with him. Without that blow, Sophie would never have prevailed. But she had helped him, with her common sense and intelligence. Henry, Jonathan reflected, had discovered what so many people must – that, as long as things do not greatly alter, within yourself, you can go on very well; but when they change profoundly, you are insecure, you are lost.

Sophie would be good to – and for – Henry. She would be firm, sensible, and loving. If she were possesive, perhaps neither Henry nor his children would realize it. She would also be an asset to the parish and a buffer between Henry and the increasing number of widows in that parish.

What Henry would be for Sophie, Jonathan didn't know. A medal, triumph, a goal, perhaps? Her own place in the sun?

He put his arm around the older man's shoulder. "I think she'll have you. I certainly hope so. Now come with me and we'll pour that sherry and then I must go to bed for I'm starting out practically at dawn tomorrow," he said.

It was an odd, half-amusing, half-pathetic hour he spent with his sister and his friend in the living room, and sherry tawny in the decanter and glasses, a little fire muttering to itself on the hearth. "So cheerful," said Henry, sighing with content, and "Takes the chill off," said Sophie. "I turned the thermostat down after the patients left."

When it was plausible to do so, Jonathan

removed himself. He said, "Don't get up for me tomorrow, Sophie. I'll be gone before Mrs. Parker comes in. You have the address and everything, and as soon as I get to that remote village I'll phone from a store or something to let you know that I've arrived safely."

He smiled, said "Goodnight, you two," and took himself upstairs, with Baffin in his wake.

His alarm went off around sunup, and Baffin yawned and got up, too. Jonathan, already packed, showered, dressed and went quietly downstairs to make coffee. But Sophie was already there and had made it. She said, when he expostulated, "I couldn't let you go off without coffee."

She looked very handsome this new, fresh spring morning and the blue of her dressing gown matched her eyes.

"Well, thanks," said Jonathan, "but you've projected a long day for yourself."

"I don't think so. Besides, I have something to tell you."

"I know." He went around the table and kissed her. "Henry told me," he said.

"But he couldn't have; that is, he hadn't —"

"He did," Jonathan interrupted. "And after I tactfully withdrew, I was sure everything would be settled. As for telling me first in the office, he was merely asking my approval."

Sophie said, "I've never been so happy, but I'm troubled about you, Jonathan."

"I'll get along," he told her. "When are you planning to be married?"

"We thought in May. By June, Henry couldn't possibly get away even for a short trip."

"I see."

"By the time you come home," she told him, "we will have made all the plans and arrangements." She flushed, looking astonishingly young. "Henry thought the Bishop might marry us. And you," she asked anxiously, "you'll give me away?"

"Dear Sophie," said her brother, "you know I'll never give you away." Then he laughed and said, "Of course."

Sophie said, "Meantime I'll look around for someone to take over the office. I could even train her."

"I've had my eye," said Jonathan, "on a gal named Winnie Foster."

Sophie said, affronted, "What do you mean?"

"Only that I've thought for some little time that eventually you'd desert me. Winnie's a good nurse. She's not young, so don't raise your eyebrow. Incidentally, do you realize your left eyebrow is slightly higher than your right, because of raising it so often? Winnie's been on private duty in homes and at the hospital for the last ten years. I heard a while back that she'd like an office job. She had one once in New York, and she lives just over the town line, so it's all quite feasible."

Sophie said, "I don't know her — at least I don't think so. But she sounds right."

In her present euphoric state, thought Jonathan, she'd have accepted the suggestion that Lucrezia Borgia preside over his office.

He pulled her to her feet, patted her firm shoulder. He said, "I'm very happy for you, Sophie. You deserve a reward."

He thought: She'll do. For the rest of her life, or his, she'll be all that Henry needs. She won't make demands on him — in the sense of demands he wouldn't want.

Sophie came with him to the car. It was a very cool morning and she'd flung their mother's shawl about her shoulders. Jonathan remembered it, from childhood.

"I'm not the shawl type," his mother would protest, when her husband would say, "Fetch your mother's shawl, someone." It was white cashmere, yellowed with the years, but it had miraculously escaped the moths. Sophie kept it in the hall closet, in a drawer of the old chest set against the wall there. She was not given to flights of imagination, but sometimes when she

278

put it on, it was like an arm about her shoulders – her mother's firm, unsentimental embrace – brief and loving.

"Have a good trip," said Sophie, radiant. "Be sure to call me."

"I shall. Give my love and blessing to Henry, although the latter is more in his department than mine."

He and Baffin drove off, and Sophie stood a moment looking after them. In a manner of speaking it was the end of an era. She went back into the house and put the shawl away, smoothing it with her long fingers. When Mrs. Parker came, there would be news for her. There was no reason to keep the plans secret until the formal announcement. She thought: Mrs. Parker will have a moment of rejoicing.

Also she'd look after Jonathan and if this Winnie whatever her name was worked out, everything would be satisfactory, and Sophie could come over often and see that it was. Henry understood her responsibility and she his.

Later she would telephone him and deliver Jonathan's message. Sitting before her dressing table, brushing her abundant fair hair, she thought of her brother. She thought: He won't really miss me. She thought, further, that she did not look her age, and that she was glad she was younger than Henry Stiles.

She wondered what Jonathan was thinking. . . .

He was not thinking of her or of anything in particular except the promise of this morning and his awareness of a sense of freedom which was, he knew, illusory. He would escape nothing for the next two weeks except routine, emergencies, and the proximity of people.

Baffin was wondering: What goes on here? He hunted carefully, with his nose, for the familiar bag which always rode in the car with them. He even peered over the back seat. The bag was associated with broken journeys; it held interesting, complicated smells. Today it was nowhere to be discerned.

On the way to a village called Stone's River they made several stops — once for gas and once, turning off the traveled road to a winding emptier one, to permit Jonathan to stretch his long legs and Baffin to explore. Passing through a town, Jonathan bought a container of milk, some sandwiches and chocolate bars. Baffin was extravagantly fond of chocolate. After that they looked for a place in which to lunch and, by following signs, found a small, seasonally deserted picnic area, with, as a result of the winter's snow, a brook galloping through it. During a drought it probably walked, brown and cold, over the rocks. Here, Jonathan stopped, took their lunch from the car and Baffin's personal table setting. He put Baffin's food in the pan and poured a dollop of milk over it. While Baffin ate, so did Jonathan, sitting on a flat sun-warmed stone, looking at budding swamp maples, and at the hills; regarding the tapestry of greens in the clustered pine and spruce, juniper, cedar and firs; watching the white and silver birches bend to the wind. The deciduous trees he'd seen on the way up were just beginning to think about leaves.

It was very still, except for the wind's whisper in the boughs. If you listened, you'd hear a needle drop. There were birds tuning up, rehearsing spring arias, and squirrels jumping about in the trees and rustling through thick carpets of last autumn's leaves. The brook sang a muted song on its way to creek and river and, ultimately, the sea.

In the later afternoon they reached the village nearest the Banning cabin. The village was small and clung to the hills like a barnacle, and the river ran through it. Jonathan did a little exploring. He had seen farms, as he came in, valley farms. Sometimes the barns were connected with the houses. There were stone walls and rocky pastures and men going about their important business without undue haste.

He'd been lost only twice on the trip after he left the main road. On the occasion he'd halted to inquire of a man sitting on a stone wall: "Can you tell me the way to Stone's River?" And the man had replied with simple veracity, "Yes."

Exact directions were obtained by asking the rational question, which was: "Will you tell me the way to Stone's River?"

Sometimes, Jonathan reflected, the Coolidge tradition was overdone.

In Stone's River the main street offered a general store, a drugstore, a gas station, and a firehouse. Jonathan saw two churches, a school, and houses set back from the street, some old, some really ancient. There was a lot of gingerbread and iron work about, also iron stags and newly painted furniture in front yards as well as cement urns which would presently spill over with petunias or geraniums. There was also a little park, with enormous maples and elms and a picnic area, and a falling-down bandstand.

Jonathan stopped at the gas station, then walked to the general store, leaving Baffin in the car. There he bought such supplies as he would need for a day or two, and telephoned Sophie. The telephone was public — extremely so. But no one looked at him except the storekeeper, and if the few people in the store listened, they did not appear to do so.

Sophie was not at home. Mrs. Parker was. She was glad, she said, that Jonathan had arrived safely. She hoped he wouldn't catch cold.

To insure himself against being lost again he asked the storekeeper for directions to Hank Johnsen's place.

"You'll be Doctor Condit," said the lean man authoritively.

Jonathan allowed that yes, he was.

He found the Johnsen house — fields, woods, a frame structure, with hills rising in back of it. There was a white picket fence and also across one field that vanishing boundary known as the stump fence. Johnsen was out in the front yard; a big heavy man, his fair hair silvered.

Jonathan got out of the car and spoke to him, and Johnsen said, "I didn't know when to expect you. I've been up to the cabin, and laid a fire in the fireplace. You probably won't need the stove, but there's coal in the woodshed. Come on in," he said, "and meet the wife."

Mrs. Johnsen, who was comfortably fat, seemed larger than life in the little parlor; and there was a girl with her, quite young, and in the advanced stages of pregnancy. Their daughter, Hilda, they explained. Her husband was in the service.

Hilda was pretty, and she had the half-frightened, half-resigned expression not unusual in her situation.

Sitting in the parlor, Hank explained that there was electricity in the cabin. "There's a hot water heater," he said. "You needn't be scared to drink the water. It's good water. Comes from a driven well. A lot of surface wells went dry last summer, but not Doc's artesian. Doc, when he phoned, said I wasn't to bother you, but if you need anything, I'm not more than two miles away. I go into town every day. I could get you anything you wanted. I put some milk and eggs in the refrigerator, and some home-smoked bacon. Didn't know if you'd stop for supplies."

Jonathan said he had, but that he'd forgotten about bacon. He didn't say he had milk and eggs.

"Better eggs," said Johnsen, "than you can buy in the store. . . . The wife's hens."

Jonathan put a hand in his pocket and Johnsen said quickly, "No need of that. . . . I'll stop by now and then and see how you're making out."

Jonathan rose and shook hands all around and Mrs. Johnsen, darting away with remarkable speed for anyone as heavy, returned with a paper bag. "Cookies," she said. "Just baked 'em."

Johnsen walked with Jonathan to the car. He

said, "That's a nice dog." and Baffin beamed.

"Well," said Jonathan, "I'm very grateful to you, Mr. Johnsen."

"Hank," said Johnsen. "Me and Doc are old friends. . . . When he sends folks up here I try to look after them."

Jonathan found the Banning cabin without difficulty by following the same road, which roughened as it moved away from the Johnsen place. There was a sign which read "Banning," and there he turned and jolted over a road even rougher, just a clearing through the trees, and one car wide. There was another clearing around the cabin, which was built of logs with the bark left on. There was also a species of carport, that is to say a roofed area with side walls but no door. He put the car in, leaving his supplies, and he and Baffin took a look around before entering the house. First they walked about the wide porch which ran around the building. At the back the land fell away; you looked downstairs to a pond, tear-shaped and colored by the declining sun; then you looked upstairs to hills and sky.

They went down the porch steps to the steep stony path leading to the pond and, halfway down, a wooden bench.

When Jonathan finally used the big key to open the door, the dusk was violet on the hills, a lingering ribbon of gold trailed across the sky, and the stars were changing guard.

The cabin was one very big room, with two little ells leading from it. There was a double couch bed; a couple of bunks; some worn, comfortable chairs; the fireplace, and the pot-bellied stove. The kitchen ell had sink and work counters, a small range, and a refrigerator. Off the woodshed there was a chemical toilet and a shower.

By the far windows, a big rough pine table evidently used for mealtimes. Cupboards and counters were at hand. There was an old-fashioned hanging lamp over the table and other lamps were glass; old but converted to electricity. Jonathan, having brought in his duffle bag, began looking into cupboards. Baffin, bored, lay down on a rag rug and slept. He woke to find that Jonathan had set the table with the ample, if unmatched china and steel utensils he'd found. He was cooking bacon and eggs and sliced potatoes in an iron spider. Coffee perked on a burner.

All the necessities, if not the luxuries, Banning had said, and Johnsen had told Jonathan that "it cost Doc a pretty penny to run the wires in."

But the power must fail often, thought Jonathan, having found a number of unconverted —

would you say heathen? — lamps in the wood-shed, their wicks trimmed. There was also kersone there, a small kerosene stove, half a dozen flashlights, a box of candles, and brass candlesticks.

When Baffin had had his after-dinner coffee — he liked it with cream and sugar — Jonathan washed up, yawning. He took the corduroy cover off the bed and tested the mattress with his hands. It was a good bed. He hadn't encumbered himself with Baffin's basket, but the rag rug would do.

Jonathan took a shower and went to bed, raw. The night was cold, but there were plenty of blankets at hand, even an old one for Baffin.

There was a sense of complete peace in the room. It was quiet, except for Baffin's occasional woofing, the calling of the wind, and the scurrying of small animals. Just before he slept Jonathan thought he heard a fox bark, but was not sure. He thought: Too early for peepers here, heard the drowsy speech of an awakened bird . . . and went to sleep.

Chapter Eighteen

The days flowed one into the next; sunup and sundown, dusk and night, and long sunny hours. Sometimes the hills wore a pearly mist, sometimes the gray feathering of fog; now and again, there was rain, a hard shower, a swift clearing; one day, all day, the drumming of rain on the roof, the dripping from the trees.

Jonathan had brought books with him. He'd had a number given him at Christmas and at other times. Now he could read. Some held his interest, others he tossed aside. He slept a good deal, lying down on the old sofa on the porch after lunch, or sometimes before dinner; any time he wished. No clocks here, only his wrist watch. He did not have to measure anything by time; he ate when he pleased, he slept when he needed sleep. Baffin seemed content to follow the leader.

They went for walks, half falling down the path to the pond, which was bigger than Jonathan had thought, and usually intensely blue.

Trees grew to the edge, but Banning's summer guests probably swam there, for there was a path cut to the water. Jonathan would sit and skim flat stones over the surface, and Baffin, of course, went swimming.

The hills around, the mountains beyond, held lovely gradations of color, always changing. And the world did not intrude. Jonathan had not even brought a battery radio. He had no need to go into the village. Once a day, usually toward evening, Hank rattled up to see if Jonathan wanted an errand done, or to bring whatever he'd asked for. Hank never stayed longer than to say, "Hello, anything I can fetch for you?"

During the first week Jonathan thought about Sophie and Henry Stiles. He thought sorrowfully about Olive Evans, and with a curious sort of homesickness of Frances. Had she returned to Seascape? he wondered. Yes, of course; and when he went back he would see her. Half his heart seemed to accelerate at the thought, and the other half to slow down, as if with a heavy uneasiness.

He thought a great deal about Edna, remembering the days of their courtship and of their brief marriage. He could not visualize her wholly, but only in flashes — an expression, a tilt of the head, a look of tenderness, a look of inquiry. Sometimes he could reproduce her voice in his mind's ear, but not often. Occasionally he could close his eyes and see her walking away from him, as he had in dreams, with her quick, light step.

Experiencing a short, happy marriage is like starting a book, putting it down, and never finding it again. How did it come out? you wonder. The happy ending, the unhappy, or the in-between? But you never find out.

Jonathan had known a good many happy marriages; there are more than most people think, since they never make headlines. His parents' had been one; it had lasted as long as they had, despite his father's volatile temperament, the exacting demands of his profession, and his quick temper which he left at home and never took on house calls, to his office, or to the hospital.

He had also known many routine unions which went in a pedestrian, mainly satisfactory manner down the long hill.

At the beginning of a happy marriage there is blinding stardust; discoveries, all lovely; wonder and radiance. Observations tell you that eyes clear; discoveries, while they may not cease, are not always lovely; wonder fades and radiance dims. These alterations are called by a variety of names, such as adjustment, maturity, growth and the realization (slow or fast) that romantic love is not the whole pattern, merely the first glittering thread.

What he had bitterly resented and regretted since Edna's death was they'd not been permitted to see the whole pattern, to know the entire story, to its conclusion, however it might have ended.

Now his marriage was a dream from which he had painfully wakened and, sleeping again, had tried to dream over.

It was time, he thought, walking the spring woods with Baffin, to let Edna go, to exorcise her small and loving ghost, to set her — and himself — free. Not to forget her — never that, even if he lived to be a very old man — but to cease to employ her as armor, as a shield against loving again, and to stop asking the questions for which there were no answers: Why? What if she hadn't fallen that icy winter day? How would it have been with us now? In ten years? In twenty?

He had assured himself that work was the narcotic, the peace-bringer, the destroyer of grief (and he'd told other people that when they had come to him in various extremities). But it hadn't proven so for him. It was still, as it had been since he graduated from medical school, a blaze of excitement; a satisfaction and also

291

a dissatisfaction, because of his impatient longing to know more, to become more. But work
had not bestowed upon him invulnerability, or
that inner sense of security which, by this, he
should have found.

He thought: Must I give so much of myself?
One is not required to give more than the skills
he has learned, the knowledge he has acquired,
and as much understanding as possible. Is it, he
wondered, because I want something in return?
Not gratitude certainly, but perhaps the recognition of myself as indispensable – which no
man is, but all, he believed, wish to become.

Sitting by the pond, walking in the woods or
along rough roads, he thought of the patients to
whom he'd gone, or who had come to him over
the years. They were like falling snow, each
flake a variation of the other. You had to look at
people closely to see any difference: those who
start with dislike and distrust, and change to
liking and dependence; those who begin
with liking and confidence, which alters and
wears away; those who begin by leaning on you
and then learn to stand by themselves; those
who lean too hard, too long. And few to whom
you can bring comfort and easing beyond their
physical needs, for whom you stand ten feet
high, for whom you are a minor god walking
among lesser men.

All this he had come to comprehend and yet he was still vulnerable.

On this particular night, he lay long awake, slept at last without dreaming, and was awakened by the sound of a car rattling over the road, a horn blowing, and then a violent knocking on the door — which was not locked — and Hank's voice calling, "Doc, Doc."

Jonathan got out of bed, swung the door wide and looked at the distraught face of Hank Johnsen.

"It's Hilda," Hank said, "she's been taken bad."

Jonathan dressed, swiftly asking questions. "What about her doctor?"

"Down sick, they took him to the hospital last night."

The hospital, Jonathan knew, was over twenty miles distant.

"When is the baby due?"

"About three weeks . . . Doc, for God's sake hurry."

Jonathan spoke to Baffin. He said, "Stay," took a heavy jacket from a hook, and followed Hank out to the car.

He said, "If we can get her to the hospital . . ."

"There just ain't time," said Hank.

Jonathan said, "Wait a minute." He ran to his

293

own car and fumbled in the glove compartment. There was a block of prescription pads there.

"What happened?" he asked, when they were on their way.

She'd slipped, on the steps, after supper. She hadn't thought anything about it, nor had they, until later.

"How close are the pains?"

Hank told him; Hilda's mother had timed them.

Dear heaven, Jonathan thought, if there are complications . . . He had no instruments with him, not even the black bag.

Jonathan went into the house and spoke to Hilda — young, afraid, and in grinding pain — and to Mrs. Johnsen. He asked for sheets and paper towels if they had them, boiling water, a pair of scissors — yes, those would do — boil them up. String also to be boiled . . . oh, and a bucket.

Hank called the druggist at his house and Jonathan talked to him, and gave him a list of what he would need, argyrol for one thing, drugs. He said, "Hank will meet you at the shop."

He told Hank, "He'll open up. You get down there, and he'll put the order together. You bring it back." He signed the prescription blanks he'd written, and went to speak quietly to Hilda. Then he scrubbed and so did Mrs. Johnsen, saying, "I can help." The strong soap and water nearly took the skin off their hands.

Hilda was young, strong, with good pelvic measurements, and she was in active labor.

Her mother gave her a folded towel to bite on, and later her own hands to hold and pull.

By the time Hank returned, it was nearly dawn. He came in, sweating, with the things Jonathan had ordered, some of which were no longer needed. Hilda's baby was a husky boy. She looked at him, bright pink and wrinkled, and smiled. The placenta had been delivered, she was no longer in pain; now she could sleep.

Mrs. Johnsen had charge of the baby. The oil Hank had brought with him was not at the moment necessary; he had been cleaned with salad oil.

"All he needs is vinegar and lettuce," said Jonathan, straightening up against a door. His back hurt. Hilda's bed was low.

A little later on this dawning day the village ambulance would transfer Hilda and her son to the hospital. Now she should sleep, but Jonathan would stay there in the spare room in case she didn't.

Hank said, over strong black coffee laced with whisky, "Dunno what we'd have done if you hadn't been here."

"Mrs. Johnsen would have managed," said Jonathan and the tired woman nodded. "Could be," she said. "Isn't the first time I've helped a baby into this world. But I'm glad you came."

He was too. Every now and then, lying on the spare bed, with the door open, after futile attempts to make Mrs. Johnsen rest, he kept thinking: Suppose there'd been complications?

Well, there hadn't been.

Noon or later, after a mammoth meal — whether Mrs. Johnsen had rested or not, she could cook like an angel — Mrs. Johnsen went to the hospital in the ambulance with Hilda and the baby. Jonathan followed in Hank's car to see his patient safely into the hospital where there were interns, residents, and nurses, and Hilda's own doctor, aged seventy, who was, Hank said, probably raising merry hell to get out of there.

Hank had said, "You take my car. I'll walk up to the cabin and bring yours back here."

And Jonathan, climbing into Hanks' battered vehicle, said, "Feed Baffin, will you?"

He telephoned Hank from the hospital. Everything was in order. He'd even looked in on old Doctor Simpkins to make a personal report. "He said she might have waited till he got home," Jonathan said.

When he got back to the Johnsens he had a

drink with Hank, who then saw him out to his car before going to the hospital to bring his wife home.

"Nothing for me to say, Doc," said Hank, "except thanks."

Jonathan drove back to the cabin. He was tired, but he also felt fine. Baffin, however, greeted him with marked coldness.

"Look," said Jonathan, "not my fault. Emergency. You'd have been in the way. And Hank fed you and gave you fresh water. So stop acting like a female, which you aren't."

Baffin remarked, all right, he'd forgive him, and then fell upon him in an outburst of affection.

"Needn't knock me down," said Jonathan. "I was sure at noon I'd never eat again, but I think I'll make coffee and open a can of beans."

He went to bed early and slept for ten hours, dreamlessly. When he woke, he still felt fine and he wasn't tired.

Nothing like a special delivery, he thought, cooking breakfast, to give a man a lift.

Speaking of mail, there had been just one note from Frances, a sprawled postcard from Roger Banning: "How are you making out?" and one short letter from Sophie, who hoped he was well. She'd never been busier. Phones, people, excitement, and wedding arrangements to make. The office hadn't been particularly busy, and Doctor Banning had everything in hand. "But people keep asking when you're coming back." She and Henry had decided to fly to Bermuda for their brief wedding trip. Everything was in such confusion. She added that Frances hadn't returned to Seascape as yet; no one had heard a word from her.

Toward the end of his second week in Stone's River there was a fire during the night in an old barn at an outlying farm. Jonathan had not heard the whistle blow, but Hank came rattling up as he had the previous week. This time he just wanted to know if Jonathan wanted to go the fire? The volunteer fire department was small, but everyone turned out.

Baffin rode with Jonathan. He'd stay in the car and give his advice to any passer-by who asked for it.

The fire had started in the hayloft, where there was some old hay. The problem was to keep it from spreading, and the house from catching. There were no hydrants. But the equipment was good and very modern. Hank was very proud of it.

All the able-bodied men were there, and Jonathan worked with them. They could not save the barn, but the house was spared.

Afterward everyone crowded into the big kitchen or sat on the porch steps to be served coffee and doughnuts. Jonathan dressed a few minor burns; one was his own.

Jonathan sat with them and listened to the discussion of chemicals, and someone said, "My day off. Guess I'll hang around to be sure."

The big hose snaked from the tank truck of water to the barn, had also kept the roof of the house watered down.

The farmer's wife said wearily, "Well, thank God, and you boys, we didn't lose the house," and the farmer, looking at the charred remains of the barn, the fallen beams still smoldering, remarked, "The insurance won't cover it."

So there was a discussion. Once the wreckage was cleared away, there'd be a barn-raising. He had, in the time it took to drink a mug of coffee, offers not only of help but of wood, hardware, and other necessary items.

It was sunup, rosy on the hills, when Jonathan followed Hank back to his house for breakfast. And Hilda, just home from the hospital and busy with the baby said, shyly, "Mind if we name him after you, Doctor?"

"I don't think your own doctor would like that," Jonathan said, smiling. "It wasn't his fault that he wasn't here, Hilda."

"I know," she said. "We'll call him Oscar, after

Doctor Simpkins, but he can have a middle name, too."

"Oscar Jonathan's a mouthful," Jonathan remarked.

"How about Condit?" asked Hank. "If you don't object."

So Oscar Condit Gillan it would be, but Jonathan inquired uneasily, "What about your husband, Hilda?"

She said, smiling, "He hates his given name — Elmer. I like it all right, but the kids in school always called him Ellie."

Chapter Nineteen

Jonathan drove home through the lovely morning. Baffin was asleep; he'd had plenty of excitement and was worn out. And Jonathan thought: I'll be sorry to leave Stone's River.

The village had given him rest and peace and time for long thinking. What if you don't arrive at hard and fast conclusions? You can think things through up to a point even if you don't solve them or reconcile yourself to some of your thoughts. Stone's River had accepted him without curiosity; and he'd felt a part of it — delivering Hilda's son, fighting with the men of the village to save a farmer's barn. The farmer's name was Stone, and Jonathan wondered if he was a descendant of the original Stone for whom the village and the river had been named.

When he reached the cabin, the sun was brilliant and it shone upon a canary-colored convertible, pulled up in the clearing, and upon the silver-gold hair of Frances Lawson, who was sitting on the porch steps smoking a cigarette. Beside her was a large clamshell, one of the many Roger Banning had provided for use as ash trays.

"Hi," said Frances, without moving.

Jonathan got out of the car, and Baffin roused, leaped out, and went to say good morning to an old friend.

"Hello, Buster," said Frances.

"I've told you he doesn't like to be called out of his name," said Jonathan, mildly stunned. He was conscious of the small bandage on his wrist, and wondered if his face was dirty. . . . It was.

"How do you know?" Frances inquired. "He's perfectly aware that when I call him Mac or Buster or Noel Coward, they're pet names and just between us. . . . You look bushed."

"I've been fire fighting. Barn."

"Had breakfast?"

"In spades, at a neighbor's."

"Come and sit down. I've already inspected the Banning villa." She indicated the ash tray. "Made myself some coffee — there's some left if you want it — and used the elegant powder room."

"Be my guest," said Jonathan.

He sat down on the steps beside her and

Baffin went off to see what was going on in the bushes.

"I stopped at a gas station," said Frances, "to ask directions and heard all about how you delivered a baby last week."

"That's right . . ."

"And now a volunteer fireman? Can't you stay out of trouble? I thought you came up here to rest."

"I did. I have rested. How did you find me?"

"It was easy," said Frances. "I asked Sophie where you'd gone and she said to Doctor Banning's hideout. So I asked Doctor Banning. I know him slightly from the hospital job."

"And what did you tell him?"

"That I might be just passing through the state."

"He believed that?"

"Of course not. He gave me a knowing sort of look; his eyebrows twitched, and the corners of his mouth. Nice guy, Roger Banning. He also gave me a map and remarked that, just in case I was within yelling distance, I might stop and see how you're getting on."

"Well," said Jonathan with resignation, "if I didn't know Roger, I'd figure that your little safari into the hills would be an interesting item over clam chowder."

"Would you care?"

"Not at this point." He smiled at her and her heart performed acrobatics. He said, "Darned if I'm not glad to see you."

"Well," said Frances practically, offering him her cheek, "prove it. Kiss me good morning. Mac — that is to say, Baffin, has."

Jonathan kissed the proffered cheek and Frances asked, "Dieting?" So he kissed her again, not on the cheek. Baffin came out of the bushes, looked at them, shook his head and went away.

"Like it here?" Frances asked. She lighted another cigarette and offered him one. They sat in companionable sun-spangled silence, with the fragrance of pines about them, and a wide blue sky above.

"Yes."

"Want to move here?"

"Lord, no," said Jonathan, "I belong in Seascape now."

"Bet there are times when you think you don't."

"Not exactly, though there are moments when it crowds me a little. This place, of course, is smaller, but as hemmed in by hills as Seascape is by water. I've made a good friend here." He told her about Hank Johnsen. "I think I'll come back now and again. I've made some good acquaintances, too. And I've been accepted — it only takes one baby and one fire."

After a moment he asked, "Where are you on your way to?"

"Never end a sentence with a preposition. Oh, here," she said. "I drove to Seascape from the city, stayed overnight to talk to Sophie and Dr. Banning, and came on. Got here last night and stayed in a motel outside of Stone's River." She told him the name of the town. "It was too dark to go cruising around these roads at night, so I waited."

"Why did you come, Frances?"

"To see you, and tell you the news."

"What news?" he asked, with some apprehension. "Your mother?"

"No. She'll be all right, they tell me. She wasn't exactly co-operative at first. She's being more so, now."

"Your father, then?"

"He's fine. He adores being sorry for himself. My aunt Charlotte is good for him. She coddles. She thinks he's America's number one brother. After all, she's considerably younger, and he, as soon as he was making a little money, took her and his parents out of the place in which they were living and gave them a decent apartment. Later he sent Charlotte through school and college and gave her a bang-up wedding to a decent, dull gentleman who is, as they say, well fixed. She has kids, but when she heard of the present predicament, she deserted her flock, put in a practical nurse, and flew East to hold Big Brother's hand. He likes it fine."

She yawned. She added, "Sorry, it's a long drive from Seascape. I'd have done better to fly up right from the city, but I first had to find out where you were. . . . Well, to return to the gossip — your sister's getting married."

"I already know that."

"But not that she looks ten years younger, and I saw Dr. Stiles when I saw her."

"Does he look ten years younger?"

"No, just bewildered, but on the whole, I think, content. Seascape sounds like a hive of friendly bees. I understand all the unattached women in Dr. Stiles's parish, and a few of the semi-attached are ready to flay Sophie's skin from her person."

"That figures," said Jonathan, smiling.

She said, "Your little friend Olive Evans has vanished from the no-doubt flinty bosom of her family."

"I know that, too."

"And Sam Karlin has also departed?"

Jonathan nodded.

"There's a rumor that they've been seen

306

together . . . somewhere." she said vaguely, "Midwest, Deep South, I wouldn't know. And also that Kim Sylvester is about to take a wife."

"Sophie told me some wealthy woman was interested in him."

"Did she tell you he'd sent you a painting?"

"No. Did he send you one, too?"

"He did. Mine is beach, palms, gulls and stuff and so is yours. Brother and sister jobs. Both, I think, very good. I wonder where we'll hang them," she said dreamily.

Jonathan got to his feet. He said, "Come take a walk, then I'll let you have a nap while I fix lunch."

So they walked along the rough trails and through the woods and down the path to the pond and Baffin came with them. Jonathan skipped stones and Frances sat on an outcrop of rock and lifted her face to the sun.

"Nice place for a honeymoon," she commented. "Think Roger Banning would let us have it?"

He said, "I'm sure he would . . . if we asked him."

"We could start now," she suggested.

"Asking?"

"No."

He took her hands, pulled her to her feet, and held her for a moment. He said, "It's not very flattering; you're yawning again."

"It's the air," said Frances. "No, it's me. I didn't sleep last night. I thought maybe you'd throw me out."

"Not yet," said Jonathan.

They went back to the cabin, and Jonathan said, "Curl up with a good book or something but with your face to the wall. I'm going to shower and change."

He smelled of smoke.

She curled up obediently, and promptly went to sleep; so did Baffin, on the rag rug.

Lunch was scrambled eggs, cold ham, potato chips, some of Mrs. Johnsen's pickles, milk for Frances, ale for Jonathan and a plate of Mrs. Johnsen's cookies.

"Gourmet's delight," said Frances. "I've never had a better meal."

He looked at her across the table. She was wearing a pale yellow skirt and pullover, her lovely legs were bare and her small feet in elkskin shoes. There was a silver chain around her neck, and something swung from it.

"What's that," he asked, "around your neck?"

She pulled the chair up so he could see what was fastened to it — a new silver quarter. "Good luck charm," she said. "I loathe sentimental women, don't you?"

"No," said Jonathan. "They are, of course,

308

rather out of fashion, but I like them."

A car came crashing along and Jonathan said, "That'll be Hank," rose and went to the open door. Hank came in, saying apolegitically, "Didn't know you had company, Doc."

"Just one of the family," said Jonathan and made the introductions.

"Bring Mrs. Lawson by for supper," said Hank. "The wife would be glad to see her and so would Oscar Condit."

"Oscar who?" said Frances.

"My grandson," said Hank, with the widest smile she'd ever seen.

"We'll be along," said Jonathan.

When Hank had gone, Frances asked, "Must we?"

He said, "Until you've tasted Mrs. J's cooking, you ain't never lived. I've put on five, ten pounds."

"On you it looks good," said Frances. "Where do the Johnsens live?"

"Two miles nearer the village."

She said thoughtfully, "You were going to suggest I take my car and you yours. Then, having my car, I'd be on the way to the motel beyond Stone's River."

"You've no right to read my mind."

"I suppose not. But I don't think I'll be going back to the motel," said Frances. "I told them not to expect me tonight. I left a small suitcase there in case they'd worry. I brought a flight bag, hopefully."

He said, "Frances, you're really —"

"Oh, don't say it," said Frances. "This is neutral ground. It isn't my house and it isn't yours; just Roger Banning's."

Jonathan said, "I've been quite aware of that ever since I saw that spectacular car sitting in the clearing."

She said, "Well, I'll wash up. You go sit on the porch and think things over. I'm sure you'll need to."

"Preposition," he reminded her, and went out and sat awhile with Baffin beside him.

Frances came out of the cabin. She'd found an apron somewhere; now she untied it and threw it over the railing. She sat down, with her chin in her hands. She said, "You don't have to marry me, Jon."

"I know. But I don't like hide and seek, and button, button, and creeping off by different routes to some public dwelling which regards Mr. and Mrs. John Q. Smith on the register without a quiver."

"I wouldn't like it either. If you married me," said Frances, "there'd be all sorts of fringe benefits and subsidiary rights."

"Yes. I won't be a very good husband. I

wasn't, I suppose, to Edna. . . ."

"Can you talk about her, now?"

"Why yes," said Jonathan.

"What was she like? I've seen her picture, of course. I sneaked into your room a time or two last Christmas."

He said, "She was prettier than that, but not chocolate-box pretty; not magazine illustration, either; not classic. Just young, and with a sort of inner radiance. She was intelligent and seeking, but not, I think, what people call clever. She made very few demands — none, in fact. Had she lived, she might have. Had she lived she might not have been as happy as she was when we were married. I would have worked harder, and longer hours, and she'd have seen less of me."

"She would have adjusted," said Frances. She put her hand over his. She said, "I'm sorry, Jon — for you and for me, too."

"Why?"

"The dreams broken off, the unfulfillments, the lack of completion."

He said, "I've thought that, too — that I'll never know now how the story would have ended."

She said, "Most women, and some men play second fiddle to a dream, Jon. I'd take that chance. You won't have to. With Charlie it was all people, pearls, and places; planes and ships and yachts and a little *pied-à-terres* in London, Paris, Rome, or New York. With Charlie it was a party . . . fun, at first, you didn't have much time to think about it while it was going on. There was no dream, except before I married, of how I'd look in my wedding dress and surrounded by eight attendants. I looked very well. The only dream I had died when he — when he was bored to death. That's what I took to Reno to cry about, instead of weeping over Charlie. . . ."

"Frances. . . ." He put his arms about her and her silky hair brushed his cheek.

She said, "You'd better not marry me. You ought to have kids, Jonathan, two, three — good healthy kids, in and out of mischief — and the boy — there should be at least one boy — going to be a doctor someday."

After a moment he said, "I can't pretend that I'm not sorry about that, Frances. I am for you, very sorry; for myself, a little. But we could adopt children."

She said, "That's probably the oddest proposal I've ever had."

"Out of the many?"

"Oh, quite a lot," she said carelessly, and kissed him. "I'm pretty, I'm rich, I'm very amusing; also, I'm lonely. Actually," she added,

"I'd make you a good wife, Jon."

"I'll think about it," he said.

"Oh, you!" She jumped up and spoke to Baffin. She said, "I'm going for another walk. I don't want you along. Just Baffin," and turned away, but not before he had seen the glitter of tears.

When she came back, which was not until nearly dusk, Baffin looked done in and Frances' long legs were scratched and there were bits of twigs in her hair. She said, "What time is supper at the Johnsens'? I'm for the powder room."

She combed her hair, washed her face and hands, reddened her lips. She thought she was singing, but she was not uttering a sound. She thought: If I'm dreaming, never let me wake. She thought: I love him so much.

She hadn't said it, really; just, long ago, that she was in love with him. That's something else again; but when you can love and be in love, it's the world in the palm of your hand, the moon in your mirror, the stars in your breast.

In the cabin the lamps were lighted and Jonathan had also brushed his hair and put on his last clean shirt. And Frances said, "We'll go in your car and leave mine here."

"As you wish," he said gravely, and then, "You're sure?"

"Of course, I'm sure. I love you. I hope you love me."

His eyes crinkled with laughter, but his smile was shatteringly sweet. He had said, "I love you," and it was not an echo of the many times he had said it to Edna. He did not repudiate that; he never would; but this was a new sound, and for Frances only.

"So unsuitable," she said, drawing away from him. "Remember — I'm spoiled, divorced, a law unto myself. . . ."

"I remember."

"You should marry someone like Sophie."

"God forbid!"

"Or, Olive Evans, a nice, quiet girl, quite suitable."

"Olive," said Jonathan, "is as domineering as Sophie. She has a passion for putting everyone's house in order. There are untidy corners of mine I'd just as soon were left alone."

"I'll leave them alone," said Frances. "Everyone is entitled to untidy corners." She looked at him, standing an arm's length away and added, "You don't have to go down on your knees and confess."

"There's nothing that you'd mind."

She thought she would always mind Edna a

314

little. But no one else. Yet Edna was a child, she thought. I'm not.

She said, "I've nothing either," and looked at him with the clear dark brown eyes, as near to black with excitement as brown eyes can be. "Since Charlie, I've never — though I've been tempted to, at times."

He said, "Forget it. I know you haven't."

"Who told you?" she demanded. "I thought it was such a well-kept secret."

"Instinct," he answered, smiling, "and also, in her own way, your mother."

"My mother! What did she say? When did she say it?"

"Oh, when I saw her at Driftwood — after her hospitalization; when she sent you and Sylvester out of the room. Among other things she said, and I remember it clearly: 'Frances is her own mistress, and hasn't, to my knowledge, ever been anyone else's.' "

"She was right," said Frances, "despite my interesting reputation. But we'll soon fix that. Every girl should have a little premarital experience, or so I've heard."

They were laughing when they went, hands clasped, to his car, put Baffin in the back seat and drove to the Johnsens.'

Frances admired the Johnsen house — not extravagantly; she was far too astute for that.

315

But she did extravagantly admire Hilda's baby and his grandmother's cooking. Each was superb.

Hilda looked at their guests and wanted to cry. She had not seen her young husband since he'd been sent to Germany. And the Johnsens looked at Jonathan and Frances and smiled because they liked to see people as God meant them to be – happy.

Afterward they went back to the cabin, and as they pulled in, he asked again, "You're sure you're sure?"

And she said, "I am. . . . Wait till I get my flight bag."

When he had fetched it for her from the convertible, she said, "Now is the time for all good men to carry their girl friends over the threshold."

He lifted her in his arms; she was as light as his heart.

In the morning Frances woke first, leaned down toward the rag rug and spoke with soft authority to Baffin. She said, "Let him sleep, hear?" and went softly barefooted to the window and looked out, smiling. This was a new day, a day trembling into spring; this was a new life and a new world washed clean, and made over.

She said in her heart, ". . . Thank you!"

Later she made the breakfast coffee and Jonathan fried the eggs, burned the toast and said, "I should have shaved. This is an occasion." He added, "I've eaten so many eggs since I came here — they're so easy to fix — that I'll never look kindly at a hen."

"You happy?" she wanted to know, a little breathless.

He said, "Happier than I ever thought I could be."

She said, "Well, you still don't have to marry me, Jon."

"Henry will marry us," said Jonathan, "when we get back to Seascape, or as soon thereafter as is legally possible. But I can't take you on a trip.... I've had mine."

Frances said, "Finish it. You aren't due back till day after tomorrow, are you? I'm leaving after my second cup of coffee."

He put his own cup down and the coffee splashed on the table. "Why?" he demanded.

"Oh, I'll go home and break the news to father. He may not like it much. I suppose he'd rather I married a second Charlie. He'll want me to be married at home. I'll explain that you can't get away" — she looked at him, smiling — "and that with Mother in the sanitarium, it's much better this way. He'll have to come up and give me away; he thinks a good deal of tradition because he never had any until he was married. You stay here until your week is up and then come home and break the news to Sophie. I'll have to move in before she leaves, I'm afraid, since she isn't being married until May, but I'll manage. As a matter of fact," she added, "I'd move into a cageful of tigers if you were there."

"You won't stay till my holiday's up?" he asked.

"Oh, no," said Frances. "I'm going to give you time to change your mind. And if you do, telephone me from Hank's, reversing charges."

A little while later, as he went out to the car with her, she said, "I must remember to pick up my little dressing case at the motel and pay my bill. What's yours, by the way?"

"A silver quarter."

She took the chain from around her neck and dropped it into his hand. She said, "It was worth considerably more."

He held the coin warmed by her body and his hand closed over it a moment. Then he gave it back to her. He said, "May I put it on, Frances — as a sort of token. At the moment I can't buy diamonds in Stone's River!"

She said, as he fastened the little clasp, "Who wants diamonds?"

He held her close and kissed her and presently she said, "Let me go now, Jon — or I won't go at all."

He and Baffin watched her get into the car. She waved, leaning from the window. "There will be fireworks in Seascape, and Sophie will have a stroke."

"We can move into the guest room, until she recovers," saids Jonathan.

Frances put her car into gear. Baffin barked. She said, abstractedly — "Good-by, Mac, for a little while." Then she said, "I'll wait for the phone call, darling."

Jonathan shook his head. He said, "I would never dream of using Hank's telephone for long distance, even at reversed charges. . . . I'll see you soon."

"Good-by." she said, then, smiling, "Hello, darling . . ."

Standing in the clearing under the pines, under the radiant sun, he watched the canary-colored convertible drive away. He felt that he was — as some of his patients had thought him — ten feet tall; he felt that he was — as others had thought him — a minor god.

There was so much ahead of them — the adjusting, the working life, the personal life, the loving life. It was all ahead — the growing into understanding, the tenderness and passion, and most of all, the sharing.

This was a new dream, he thought; once a dream had been like a new moon, a sliver of silver, which had never grown into the full round. This one must become the full round, one which waned and waxed, but was always in itself complete.

Sharing. This was the keynote. He would, because of his temperament, be lonely often, but now it was a loneliness which, in a sense, he could share.